A Return to Hertfordshire

Perpetua Langley

A Return to Hertfordshire

Chapter One

Elizabeth Darcy pulled back a heavy drape and peered out of one of the tall windows that lined the drawing room at Pemberley. She watched with amusement as Darcy and Bingley strode across the lawn looking as resolute as soldiers off to war. They were determined to shoot pheasant, though Elizabeth had so little confidence in the idea that she had already spoke to cook about a saddle of mutton for dinner. Still, she knew they would both enjoy the day out and she and Jane would be perfectly happy to lend a sympathetic ear to their tales of near misses when they returned.

"What shall we do, Lizzy?" Jane asked from the sofa. She held Lydia's latest letter in her hand. "We vowed we would not send Lydia any more money, but each letter is worse than the last. In this, she writes: '*Wickham is so deranged from wont that I fear he may do a violence to himself. He says you must send money or he will leave me and we shall never hear from him again. Beloved sister, if that were to happen I would need somewhere to live and must come to you, as Bingley would be far easier to prevail upon than the great and awful Mr. Darcy.*"

Elizabeth erupted in peals of laughter over this apt description of her husband. It was true that he could present a very grave countenance when he chose, but she had learned that grave countenance was as thin and fragile as an eggshell and it encased an expansively kind heart. A thin and fragile eggshell she had been happily chipping away at for above seven months.

"Dear Jane," Elizabeth said, "Mr. Wickham can hardly do a violence to himself *and* leave Lydia at the same time. He must do one or the other. We should hardly bother discussing it until he absolutely chooses which he will do."

"I think she means to express how dire their circumstances are at present," Jane said.

"It is Mr. Wickham's own fault that he ruined his career in the Regulars," Elizabeth said. "Nobody told him to carry on gambling. Further, though you will think me mean and cross for saying so, I am sure our sister's situation is not so bad as that. Lydia is far too dramatic and I suspect what she means to say is that Wickham is inconvenienced by lacking all the finer things in life that he believes he deserves but has never spent an hour working toward. Lydia and Wickham have an allowance, kindly provided by my husband, and they can most comfortably live on it if they practice just a little economy."

"But she could not mean she would really come to me if he left her?" Jane asked with real concern in her voice. "Lydia cannot mean that. She would not impose on Bingley's good nature to such a degree?" Jane laid the letter on the table as if it carried a dreadful disease.

"Oh Jane," Lizzy said, "when will you see that our sister is a master of veiled threats. She attempts to put you in the idea that either money must be had or she will take over one of your spare bedchambers forevermore. Nonsense, all of it. Wickham will not leave her, as he would lose the allowance and then he truly would go mad from wont."

Jane seemed mollified by Elizabeth's assurances. It was early November and a chill wind blew outside. Elizabeth had left the window and the sisters sat together cozily in front of the fire. Jane and Bingley had been visiting for over a fortnight and would stay a month more. At the end of it, the sisters would travel together to Longbourn to visit their mother and father. They felt obligated to make the trip, as they would not be in attendance at Christmas. Their mother complained bitterly that they did not all come for the holiday, but Elizabeth would not subject Darcy to the aggravation that multiple dinners with Mrs. Bennet would provide. She felt well repaid for the courtesy, as Darcy would not subject *her* to the opposing invitation from Lady Catherine, which would not only provide the aggravation of the lady herself, but would be further compounded by the fawning Mr. Collins. Those Elizabeth really wished to see managed to see her at Pemberley. Her father visited when the mood struck him and dear Charlotte had already managed to come once without her husband. Relatives, Elizabeth had decided, must be carefully managed to ensure a happy marriage.

Elizabeth and Darcy laughed together often over letters received from their ridiculous relations – silliness on one side and haughtiness on the other. In the beginning of their marriage, they had maintained a quiet reserve on the subject of their respective families. They had both seemed to feel that the less said, the better. But that could not hold over time. One letter after the next arrived until finally Elizabeth found one from her mother entirely too diverting and read it aloud to her husband. Her mother had written that Mr. Bennet had taken to wanting to know what everyone was doing at all times of day and Mrs. Bennet had not yet thought up a scheme to thwart him in it and did Elizabeth have any likely ideas. That same day, Darcy received a letter from Lady Catherine that detailed all the advice she had recently given Mr. Collins. The size and placement of closets was minutely discussed and it was reported that Mr. Collins had approved every idea. Darcy commented that Mr. Collins would likely tear his house down if Lady Catherine advised such a step. Since then, it had become almost a competition to see who could reveal the silliest letter of the morning. Amusing as the letters were, they both agreed that the writers of the letters were less amusing in person.

No, for the holiday they would be at Pemberley. On Christmas Eve they would take the carriages out and visit the tenants. Darcy carried on his father's tradition of delivering gifts. Elizabeth had not been surprised by that, though she had been very surprised when she had met with Mrs. Reynolds and had been apprised of what exactly they would deliver. The Darcys gifted their tenants with everything from coins to jam to meat to wine to cloth. There would be carriage-loads to take round and after the holidays Mrs. Reynolds would begin planning for next year. Elizabeth was satisfied that her husband's generosity would provide a very happy Christmas for all who were associated with the family.

The following day they would gather round the Christmas fire, just Elizabeth, Darcy, Bingley, Jane and Georgiana. Kitty would join them after the new year. Elizabeth had almost taken Kitty directly after the wedding, as she thought it best that her sister find herself under some rational influence after being in Lydia's grasp for so long. But in the end, Elizabeth had decided that it would be best to spend time with her husband alone and cement her relationship with Georgiana without any interference. In that way, Kitty would find that she faced a united front and would have no choice but to amend her habits and ways of thinking. Elizabeth only feared that the intervening months under her mother's influence had not done Kitty any good.

Jane would not hear a word against her mother, though Elizabeth noticed that her sister somehow discovered all sorts of reasons why Bingley was never to spend much time in Hertfordshire. Jane had even gone so far as to encourage him to let Netherfield go, which he had happily and speedily done. The couple currently lived in London and looked for a house in Derbyshire that would not be too great a distance from Pemberley.

Bingley was far more good-humored than Darcy when it came to Mrs. Bennet, but even he might be caught searching for a door if an awkward conversation went on long enough. Mrs. Bennet had not improved over the intervening months since Elizabeth and Jane had got married. If her letters were anything to go by, Elizabeth thought her mother was rather worse. Having three daughters to brag of, she did not let an opportunity slip by to comment to Lady Lucas about 'poor Charlotte only married to a clergyman' and 'lucky Lydia married to the dashing Mr. Wickham' and 'rich Lizzy with as many carriages as she likes' and 'happy Jane joined to the amiable Mr. Bingley.' Mrs. Bennet proudly recounted all such conversations in her letters. There was never any mention of how Lady Lucas reacted to these pronouncements.

"I am very much afraid, Lizzy," Jane said, "that Lydia and Wickham might present themselves at Longbourn while we are there. It would be very like Lydia to think she might work on me better in person. She has no shame and will not be embarrassed to see anyone, our father and Darcy included. You know our mother has probably pressed her to come and it would not surprise me to know that she had sent Lydia some money to make the trip."

Elizabeth suppressed a sigh. She was not at all looking forward to the visit, though she welcomed the chance to see her father. She did not fear Lydia's opportuning, Elizabeth was quite up to the task of disappointing her sister. She did not quake at the thought of encountering Wickham. She knew him for what he was, and he knew she knew it. Wickham would give her a wide berth. In truth, Elizabeth did not worry on her own account at all. It was the final evening of the visit she fretted over. Darcy and Bingley would visit a friend in Essex, then they would come to Hertfordshire to collect Jane and Elizabeth to return to London before making the trip back to Pemberley. Elizabeth had argued that she and Jane were perfectly capable of making their own way up to London, but she had been overruled. Darcy swore he would rather live at Longbourn a month than have his wife and sister-in-law so inconvenienced. Elizabeth had given up. There would be a dinner, and ample time for Mrs. Bennet to say something, or many things, outrageous. Were Wickham to make an appearance, it would be so much the worse. Elizabeth knew her dear Darcy would bring all of his self-discipline to bear while visiting Longbourn, but she was also certain he would be well-vexed by the end of it. Were he forced to endure Wickham's company, he would be more than vexed.

"Do not you worry overly much, Jane," Elizabeth said. "If Lydia appears, I shall endeavor to be always nearby. Lydia knows she will not have much success if I am always listening. As for Wickham, I do not think we shall see him. He was received at Longbourn after the wedding, but I do not think he is welcome. Not by our father, at any rate."

"I do wish I had your strength," Jane said. "If Lydia makes an attempt I will feel both inclined to run from her and throw money at her before I do. Bingley is no better. He cannot bear to make anyone unhappy, not even a person he is not particularly fond of."

"Not particularly fond of?" Elizabeth cried. "You and Bingley are becoming quite the hardened characters! Not six months ago you would have both searched desperately for some kind thing to say of Lydia and finally settled on her high spirits being something to note."

"That is no doubt true," Jane admitted. "But I find my loyalty must be solely with my husband. What is unpleasant to him, must be unpleasant to me."

"Brava, Jane," Elizabeth said. "You are finally coming around to my way of thinking. Though I warn you sister, if you continue with it you will no longer see the world as filled with only goodness. You shall take on my more cynical eye and find fault with everybody."

"You know you do not do so, Lizzy," Jane said. "I fear you still blame yourself for not immediately recognizing Darcy's good character."

"There you go, falling right back into good Jane," Elizabeth said. "You know perfectly well that it was a bit more than not immediately recognizing his good character. I abused the man to all of Meryton and now I pay the price for it each time I meet an acquaintance for the first time since the wedding. How am I to account for myself? Here is Elizabeth Darcy, having recently married the man she told everyone within earshot that she despised."

"Lizzy, everyone knows there is no accounting for love," Jane said, smiling. "Nobody expects anything sensible out of it."

"I suppose you are right," Elizabeth said. "My own interesting way of proceeding has led to much happiness. I am entirely too kind to Darcy, and he to me, as we attempt to atone for a hundred insults thrown at each other during our highly original courtship."

Jane smiled but said nothing. Elizabeth thought her sister seemed not quite herself and did not think Lydia's letter could account for it. The night before, she had caught Jane staring pensively at Bingley more than once. "Jane," she said, "are you bothered by something? Is all quite right between you and Bingley?"

Jane looked up in surprise. "Whatever made you say that?"

"I do not know," Elizabeth said, "except that I know you so well that any little change must seem monumental to me."

"Oh, Lizzy," Jane said, nearly breathless. "You have sharp eyes, indeed. There is a change coming. A happy change. I am with child."

Much relieved, Elizabeth hopped up and hugged her sister. "A baby! Does Bingley know?"

"He does not," Jane admitted. "I have been wondering when I should tell him. I did not wish to tell him too early in case something went wrong. I am quite past that danger, but I think if I tell him now, he should not like me traveling to Hertfordshire."

"Quite right he would be," Elizabeth said. "What a happy excuse to avoid the trip altogether. You shall stay here and I will go and face our frightful family alone."

"But that is what I do not wish!" Jane said. "You will be at Longbourn and Darcy and Bingley will be at Hartfield and Georgiana will be with Miss Crandall in London. I have never felt better in my life and do not want to stay here alone. I should pace a hole in the carpet from boredom."

"Well," Elizabeth said, "I suppose if you feel quite well there's no harm in it."

"Precisely," Jane said. "I shall tell Bingley when we return here for the holiday."

"Ah, what a lovely Christmas gift that will be," Elizabeth said. "I sincerely hope I do not fall too far behind you with similar news."

They spent the rest of the afternoon planning the life of the coming child down to the very hour. Jane had already given it a lot of thought. If it were a boy, she would consult Bingley on what would be best, since she had never had a brother. If it were a girl, Jane was determined to hire tutors in everything – dancing, drawing, music, literature, history, languages and anything else she could think of. She was convinced that Mrs. Bennet's way of doing things, which had been to let the girls educate themselves as they might, was not the most beneficial.

Elizabeth and Jane spent much time discussing how it would be if Elizabeth would soon be with child. The cousins must become acquainted as babies and become life-long friends. They would learn to ride together and Jane and Bingley would take a house quite close to Pemberley and they would always be going back and forth.

After Darcy and Bingley returned with bags empty as expected, they had a lively dinner of roast mutton.

"I tell you," Bingley said at table, "these are not your usual pheasants. These Pemberley pheasants absolutely mock us."

"It has always been so," Darcy added with a smile. "I remember my father remarking on it. He called them the Perverse Pemberley Pheasants."

"Jane," Elizabeth cried, "we must take pity on our poor husbands. They have bravely battled birds that possess diabolical intelligence and are capable of impossible gymnastics and absolutely refuse to be killed. I am only thankful our men have been returned to us uninjured."

Georgiana looked back and forth between Darcy and Elizabeth. She was at first shocked at how Elizabeth teased her brother, but now she found it highly interesting. She did not yet dare to do it herself, but she liked to think that someday she would marry a man who did not mind being teased.

"I am glad you take my word for it," Darcy said, "or I would be forced to question my aim."

"Mine as well," Bingley said. "There was no shortage of lead flying today."

"I was quite well-prepared for the combat I knew you would face," Elizabeth said. "I ordered the mutton before you were off the lawn."

The dining room erupted in laughter and Elizabeth was sure that Jemmings and the footmen were doing their best not to laugh. They always had very pleasant dinners, but it was especially high-spirited when Bingley and Jane were there.

The trip to Longbourn went smoothly. They stopped their journey in London for two days' time so that Jane and Elizabeth might do some shopping and Georgiana could get settled. Darcy had sent two horses ahead to Longbourn. He and Bingley would accompany Jane and Elizabeth to the Bennet's in the carriages and then would continue on horseback to visit an old school friend of Darcy's. Elizabeth thought her husband very clever to have arranged it – Darcy and Bingley would not even step inside the house at Longbourn, but would be on their way immediately. Elizabeth doubted her mother would have time to insult her husband when she would only see him for a moment in the courtyard.

Now, as they rattled along the road to Longbourn, Darcy held her hand clasped in his. Elizabeth had learned that he liked always to have her hand in his, though he would be mortified for anyone else to see it. He took his opportunities where he might – in a carriage, during a walk in the garden, or when they found themselves alone in the drawing room.

"How do you do, Mrs. Darcy?" he asked.

"Very well, Mr. Darcy," Elizabeth said. "Though I rather feel as if I am about to go into battle. Is not that strange?"

"Hardly," Darcy said, laughing. "I would feel the same if we were just now barreling toward Rosings. I would not hope to find it much improved, so I suppose you cannot either."

"No," Elizabeth said, "nothing improved but my father. He has been much improved by the past year's events."

"Your father was a man of sense to begin," Darcy said. "He only wanted a clearer vision of his own role in his daughters' lives and now he has got it."

"I hope he has paid close attention to Kitty," Elizabeth said. "I have not felt entirely easy leaving her behind. Mary is quite safe; she is too attached to her books to fall into much trouble. But Kitty…"

"Kitty will soon enough be under our own roof. We will happily receive her and she will be much influenced by Georgiana. It can only do her good."

"Indeed," Elizabeth said. "Everyone must benefit by keeping company with Georgiana."

"And with you, my dear," Darcy said, "everyone must benefit by keeping company with *you*. I know I have done."

"Oh!" Elizabeth cried. "Let us not travel down that garden path again or I will be forced to acknowledge all my mistakes and you, as a gentleman, will be forced to respond with all of yours. No, sir, let us claim amnesia to all of it so that we may confine ourselves to congratulating each other on being in perfect harmony now."

Darcy squeezed Elizabeth's hand. "And so we are."

Longbourn came into view. "The battle begins," Elizabeth said ruefully.

The courtyard of Longbourn was in a clamor at the arrival of the two sisters.

"Dear Jane!" Mrs. Bennet cried. "Dear Lizzy! Our own Mr. Bingley!" She paused, then delivered a short and shallow curtsy. "Mr. Darcy."

Elizabeth blushed. She had not thought it possible, but somehow her mother had indeed found a way to be rude to Darcy in the short moments she would have with him. She glanced at her husband.

To her surprise, Darcy looked rather amused. "Mrs. Bennet," he said, smiling.

Mrs. Bennet appeared confused that her carefully aimed arrow had somehow missed its mark. Mr. Bennet came out of the house and greeted Darcy and Bingley very civilly. Her father liked both men very much and became almost social when they were nearby. He pressed them to stay until the morrow, but did not look surprised to hear that they would not.

Kitty bounded out of the house, then collected herself. Elizabeth thought it probable that Kitty was currently at war with herself. She was still inclined to run through life as Lydia had, but at the same time she had received many letters from Elizabeth on what would be right and what would be expected if she were to ever visit Pemberley. Kitty understood how close they had all come to being ruined, though perhaps did not attribute it so entirely to Lydia's impetuous nature. Elizabeth guessed Kitty was doing her best to accomplish all that Elizabeth had advised, as she no doubt wished that a visit to Pemberley might be arranged, but that it had not been easy with no example to follow and memories of good fun with Lydia still fresh in her mind.

"We shall return in two days' time," Darcy said to Mr. Bennet, "at which point we will happily accept your kind offer to stay the night."

"Mrs. Bennet sniffed and said, "I'm sure I never heard of people rushing off without coming in doors, but I suppose there is much I don't understand."

Elizabeth felt all the humor of her mother claiming that there was much she did not understand and bit her lip to hide a smile. She dared not look at Darcy as she thought if she did he might very well laugh out loud. If that statement had arrived in a letter, she and her husband would have had a very merry breakfast over it.

Jane said, "Mama, I did tell you the cause of it, remember? They must leave now if they are to reach Hartfield by sunset."

"Oh yes, you told me," Mrs. Bennet said. "Though I don't see why they are to go to Hartfield at all. But I suppose our little family is of no account to a great man."

It was apparent to Elizabeth that her mother put the full blame of their departure on Darcy's shoulders. Mrs. Bennet would not for a moment believe Bingley willing to stay away from Longbourn. Elizabeth thought the sooner the two men were on their way the less Mrs. Bennet would be able to say about it and that would be for the best.

Mr. Bennet seemed to be of the same mind and had already ordered that the horses be brought round.

Mary wandered out of the house, book in hand. Until that moment, she had been playing the pianoforte in a most determined manner. She had pried the window to the music room wide open so her mastery of the instrument could be appreciated from the courtyard. As nobody had come inside to discover who the maestro could be, she had given it up and picked up her second favorite prop – a heavy book on a ponderous subject.

"Good afternoon, sisters," Mary said. "I am glad you have come. I have learnt much since you were here last and I am determined that you shall not go away until you are equally acquainted with it. I find that there is much to be said for sharing the information one has gained through rigorous study."

Elizabeth quietly groaned. Darcy was about to mount his horse. He bent down and whispered, "Courage, my adorable soldier."

Elizabeth and Jane watched their husbands trot down the drive. It felt rather like the men had abandoned a sinking ship.

Chapter Two

Darcy and Bingley took an easy pace as they headed toward Meryton. They would pass through the town and then turn onto the post road toward Hartfield. Darcy had a stop to make in town, though he hardly knew how to broach the subject.

He cleared his throat. "Bingley," he said, "I must just stop a minute to post a letter."

"A letter?" Bingley asked, his voice full of surprise. "To who?"

Darcy did not answer. Bingley said, "Excuse me, Darcy. I should not have asked; it is certainly none of my concern."

"You might as well know," Darcy said, certain his face was red. "It is a letter to Elizabeth. Though I charge you, as my friend, to never repeat that to a soul."

"Surely not!" Bingley said. "I only wish I had thought of it. Jane will think me a careless husband when Mrs. Darcy gets a letter and Mrs. Bingley does not."

They had entered the town proper and Darcy could not help but notice the looks he received from various people on the pavement. He knew from Elizabeth what the general consensus on his character had been. He had been accused of ruining Wickham's prospects and for quite some time he was the villain of the hour. But even when that accusation was overcome and the truth about Wickham was generally known, he was still regarded as a proud and haughty man. He knew perfectly well that he had brought that on himself. He had not the natural inclination to be friendly with everybody. Elizabeth had made him see that if he would only make an effort, if he would only smile at people, he would be duly rewarded.

Darcy spotted Mrs. Philips, tipped his hat to the lady and smiled. She stared at him as if she had just seen a goblin and hurried into the milliner's shop.

It would take some time, Darcy thought ruefully, to entirely reverse public opinion of him in Meryton. All he could do was be ruled by his wife's guidance on such matters. While he was expert in managing his estate, he acknowledged Elizabeth to be the expert on social relations. Whatever she advised he would follow, and so he would keep tipping his hat and smiling.

Elizabeth and Jane found Longbourn little changed. The drawing room looked as if they had just left it, but for one addition to the room that had not been there before. Their father. Mr. Bennet had realized, after Lydia's scandalous elopement, that hiding himself in the library had left his daughters under the sole and nearly fatal influence of his wife. He fully blamed himself and had determined to prevent such a catastrophe from happening again. Mr. Bennet still retired to his library for part of the day, as he could not bear up under the harassment of Mrs. Bennet for more than an hour or two, but he made certain that if there were any plans discussed to go to Meryton or anywhere else, he would be apprised of them. He had gone so far as to limit the amount of time Kitty was permitted to spend with her aunt as he was not at all confident of who Mrs. Phillips would receive in that house or what sort of supervision could be expected from the lady.

Mr. Bennet stayed with them through tea and Elizabeth diverted him with descriptions of the various characters inhabiting the village of Lambton. There were the two bakers, Mr. Jenkins and Mr. Clyde, whose establishments sat directly across the road from each other at the center of the town. The two men engaged in a vigorous competition and Elizabeth predicted that someday a stranger in need of a loaf of bread would be pulled in half between them. As it was, the village had divided itself into two camps: the Jenkins-breaders and the Clyde-breaders. The opposing sides often hotly debated the merits of the two men's yeast and respective crusts and the village had even seen two merchants come to blows over the question.

Then there was Mrs. Helby, who claimed to know everything about every subject and if she did not know it, as she mostly did not, she would be happy to invent it. Elizabeth had recently heard that she was advising all and sundry that under-ripe apples had been positively proved to cause colds and must be avoided at all costs. This had brought her into some difficulty with a local farmer who regularly sold apples at market, but the lady had stood firm in her directive. She would not be bullied into a retreat when the health of the village hung in the balance.

Then there was Mr. and Mrs. Riderhorn, who presumed themselves to be the arbiters of fashion and good taste, though Mrs. Riderhorn had a habit of wearing so many ostrich feathers in her hat that Elizabeth was certain she should see the lady flying over Pemberley on some windy day. Mr. Riderhorn was all bluff and bluster and considered his shop to be as good as any seen on Bond Street, though he had never been to that fabled avenue and could only guess at those famous shops' inferiority to his own.

Mr. Bennet laughed heartily, as there was nothing he liked so much as tales of human frailty. He seemed genuinely pleased to have his two eldest daughters back under his roof, and especially Elizabeth as she could entertain him as no one else could.

After Mr. Bennet left the ladies to themselves, Mrs. Bennet vented all her despair at their current way of living.

"You see how it is, girls," she said. "Mr. Bennet will insist on being in here at all times of day. We never know when he is coming and it goes a great deal against our habit of having our own confidential conversations."

"Madam," Elizabeth said, "you cannot possibly oppose your husband's company?"

"Oh, do not get on your high horse, Lizzy," her mother said. "There's nothing wrong with Mr. Bennet's company. I would just wish he would keep his company where it has always been – limited to the dining room at dinner."

"But surely, mama," Jane said, "you must find it a comfort that our father has become so interested in the doings of the household."

"Comfort?" Mrs. Bennet cried. "There is nothing comfortable about it! Do you know that he has forbidden Kitty go to Meryton as often as she likes? He says he will limit how much time she spends with my sister. My own sister!"

Kitty stared at her hands. Elizabeth suspected she was deeply unhappy at the new arrangement, but that she knew that she should not be. Mrs. Phillips was in the habit of throwing a jolly party, and Elizabeth and Jane had enjoyed their share of them, but it was no place for Kitty on her own.

"I am sure that is best," Elizabeth said. "I realize that there are no soldiers about anymore, but nevertheless, that is where the whole business with Lydia began. It may have ended in Brighton, but it began in Meryton."

Kitty had the good sense to blush at the reference to Lydia's shame, but Mrs. Bennet did not.

"Lydia, as you may recall," Mrs. Bennet said, "is now married to Mr. Wickham. I'm sure I don't have a more charming son-in-law than Wickham. Except dear Bingley, Jane. Of course I would not forget Bingley."

Elizabeth ignored this slight to Darcy and said, "Lydia is lucky that is how it turned out for she was in grave danger of it turning out otherwise."

"But that *is* how it turned out and I do not see how poor Kitty is to find a husband if she is always to be locked up here."

This was the moment Elizabeth had been dreading. She had corresponded with her father about Kitty coming to live at Pemberley and he had heartily agreed. They had decided between themselves that Elizabeth would break the news of the arrangement and Mr. Bennet would field all of his wife's complaints about it. Elizabeth thought that was more than fair, since the complaints would go on long after she had departed the house.

"I have given a deal of thought to Kitty's situation," Elizabeth said.

"Good Lizzy," her mother said. "I should have known I could rely on your commonsense. Do go in to your father and reason with him. Kitty must be allowed to go into Meryton whenever she likes. She is a young girl and needs her entertainments, just as you and Jane always had."

"That is not at all the direction my thoughts have taken," Elizabeth said. "I feel it would be beneficial to Kitty if she were to come and live with me for a time."

Kitty blushed and smiled and looked away.

"Live with you?" Mrs. Bennet cried. "What shall *I* do if Kitty is to go away? Am I to sit here, quite alone?"

"I will still be here, mama," Mary said. "We might enjoy reflecting on Fordyce's Sermons together. I have often thought you might benefit from such study. I find his sermon on female virtue and intellectual accomplishment particularly illuminating. That women adorn themselves with sobriety, I believe is the beginning."

"Really, Mary," Mrs. Bennet said. "Adorn myself with sobriety? I never heard of anything more ridiculous. Fordyce, indeed."

"The arrangement would be advantageous to Kitty," Elizabeth said. "I must think you would put aside any inconvenience to yourself in an effort to better one of your daughters."

"None of my daughters needs to be any better than they are," Mrs. Bennet said. "I'm sure I don't know why it should be so beneficial for a girl to be away from her own mother. Kitty could not bear to part with me and I won't make her do it."

"But I should so like to meet Georgiana," Kitty said, sounding as if she could, indeed, bear to part with her mother for such a chance.

"I don't know why you should," Mrs. Bennet said. "If she's at all like her brother you shall find her haughty and standoffish. Not my own opinion of good breeding, but the Darcys seem to have other ideas."

Elizabeth was determined to stop her mother from going any further in abusing her husband. "It has been decided by our father that Kitty will come to me," she said firmly.

"When shall I, Lizzy?" Kitty cried.

"I shall send for you after the new year," Elizabeth said. "And Mary, I have not forgotten you. You will be next. Once Kitty is settled in some fashion I shall send for you, too. In a year or so, I should think."

Mary looked up from her book. "I would not mind viewing foreign scenes, Lizzy. I know that it is beneficial to the mind to travel. I would only hope to retain time for my studies. It would not be right to dedicate myself solely to frivolous enjoyment."

"Nobody would ever accuse you of it, Mary," Elizabeth said.

Mrs. Bennet had sat silent, appearing deeply shocked. "Mr. Bennet has already approved this scheme? How long have these conversations gone on? Why was I not consulted?"

"I suspect you were not consulted because you would not agree," Elizabeth said. "But you must know it will be the best thing for Kitty. I know you, mama, you wish to have all your daughters well-settled. What better opportunity for Kitty than that she should enjoy all the introductions Mr. Darcy can provide? How satisfying it would be for you to explain to Lady Lucas that there has been another brilliant match?"

Elizabeth had rehearsed that line of reasoning well ahead of time, though it was nothing close to the truth. She would certainly not be trotting Kitty out into society for quite some time. No, Kitty would have the best tutors that money could buy and close supervision from Elizabeth. Only after she had undergone a significant transformation and was sufficiently turned into a modest and unassuming young woman would she be permitted to meet anybody. Still, a chance at a rich husband was the only explanation that was likely to have any effect on Mrs. Bennet.

"To be sure, Lady Lucas would be green with envy were such a thing to occur," Mrs. Bennet said. "But Lizzy, I must have some company. Perhaps I should come as well. I could very well keep out of Mr. Darcy's way. He can have no more cause to seek me out than I him and I suppose it is a very big house. Mary will not mind staying behind to look after your father."

Elizabeth was momentarily frozen. Of all the arguments she had imagined her mother might pose, coming to Pemberley had not been one of them. "I'm sure our father would not agree to that," she said in as lighthearted a tone as she could muster.

"Never you mind," Mrs. Bennet said. "I'll talk to him and make him see that it's right. Oh, Kitty! What fun we should have, meeting all sorts of eligible gentleman. I don't suppose there are any officers, but that cannot be helped. I'm sure we should meet a deal of charming men."

"Mama," Elizabeth said firmly, "I must put a stop to this immediately. Mr. Darcy would never agree to it, and so I can never agree to it."

The afternoon was long after that. Mrs. Bennet by turns claimed that Kitty could not go, or that Mrs. Bennet herself *would* go and Mr. Darcy could say what he liked about it and she would see if he had the nerve to throw her out on the road or that they should all go to Brighton together, just as they ought to have done when Lydia went. Elizabeth could hardly bear to hear her mother talk of Lydia as if the girl had done nothing wrong. However, as much as it weighed on her, it was far more affecting to Jane. Jane had not her ability to shrug off the more shocking things Mrs. Bennet had to say. Finally, Mrs. Bennet said, "If we all go to Brighton, it won't be a minute before Kitty is engaged to an officer. They are still there, you know."

"I have no doubt of it," Elizabeth said, "but how should we face them? Could you really look Colonel Forster in the eye after Lydia's shameful behavior?"

"You are becoming too fine a lady, Lizzy," her mother said. "You are beginning to give yourself airs."

Elizabeth was growing angry. She knew her mother did not comprehend the seriousness of what Lydia had done, nor the ruin the girl had nearly brought them all to. To Mrs. Bennet, all was well that ended well.

"Having a good dose of understanding of social conventions is hardly giving myself airs, mama. What Lydia did was shocking and showed her to be a girl of little sense, little self-control and no morals. She came very close to, well, I will not say what she came close to. In the process, she would have carelessly ruined the lives of all of her sisters. So pardon me if I do not look at what she did lightly, or forgive it because she managed to get married, or have any interest at all of ever seeing the militia again."

Kitty looked in wonder at Elizabeth. Elizabeth suspected that this was the first time Kitty had heard Lydia's crime spelled out so plainly. She hoped it did her sister good to hear it. She knew it did no good to her mother whatsoever.

Mrs. Bennet rolled her eyes and said, "Every time I have ever complained of the entail, you have advised me to avoid thinking of what might have been, and instead think only of what is. Yet, when I do the same in Lydia's case, you are against it. You are capricious, Lizzy. I have always said so."

Jane suddenly rose. "I shall go rest for a moment. I do not feel well."

Elizabeth took her arm. "I shall take you up. I make little progress here in any case."

Darcy and Bingley trotted along the post road. They had been silent for some minutes. Quite suddenly, Bingley said, "My wife is with child."

Darcy reined in his horse. "Congratulations," he said. "Does Elizabeth know? How long have *you* known?"

"I do not know if Elizabeth knows," Bingley said, blushing. "For myself, I guessed while we were in London. I had noticed…certain things, but I did not perceive anything in it. I just thought, pleasant dinners and all that. But then I happened to see some packages she bought. Most of it was for a baby."

"But she has not told you yet?" Darcy asked.

"Not a word," Bingley said. "I suppose there is some protocol I know nothing about and she will tell me when the husband is meant to be apprised of such matters."

Darcy knew nothing of what that protocol might be, but found it interesting to think about. If Elizabeth were with child, when would she tell him? He looked forward to being a father, though he had always felt as a father already to Georgiana. A baby, that would be, well it would be wonderful.

"You have my congratulations, Bingley," Darcy said. "Most heartily."

In Jane's bedchamber, Lizzy said, "Are you indeed ill, Jane?"

"Not of body," Jane said. "I only found the conversation so taxing I could not bear another moment of it. Oh, it makes me thankful for dear Bingley."

"I am afraid I was harsh with our mother, but I find I am not so likely to have a care for her feelings as I once was. Kitty must be protected."

"To think, mama would propose coming to Pemberley after how she spoke to Darcy just this afternoon," Jane said.

"Darcy would never allow it," Elizabeth said, "and were he to lose his wits and think to allow it, *I* would never allow it. Though I must say, it might be amusing to take our mother to Rosings someday. Perhaps I will write Charlotte and ask if I may come for a visit and bring mama with me. Surely, Charlotte would agree to it. She'd instantly see how diverting such a thing would be."

"Oh you would never!" Jane said, laughing.

"If my mother thinks I give myself airs," Elizabeth said, "she would think differently were she to have tea with the great Lady Catherine. Further, one can only wonder with amusement at what Lady Catherine would make of Mrs. Bennet. Mr. Collins would be positively apoplectic at the exchanges those two ladies would likely have."

Elizabeth paced the room, taking on the air of Lady Catherine. "Mrs. Bennet," she intoned, "I understand you have had five daughters and not one governess. I find that alarming. Had you consulted me, I would have advised against it. How does one turn out five daughters without a governess?

"And now," Elizabeth said, "our mother's response. She would stare straight at Miss de Bourgh and say, 'I'm sure I don't see how it helps so very much.'"

"I should not laugh, Lizzy, I know I should not. I cannot help it. I feel quite cheered now, and ready to face anyone."

Dinner passed with no mention of the plan to send Kitty to Pemberley, though listening to her mother's peevish comments throughout, Elizabeth was sure that her father had stood firm on the idea.

"I suppose I am to be here quite alone," Mrs. Bennet said to the air. "I don't suppose there is any reason why anybody should take *my* feelings into consideration. Nobody ever has before. That I suffer from a nervous condition is something I must bear up against quite unassisted."

Kitty did not dare comment, though Mary did. "Mama," she said, "I think you bring the nerves on yourself. If you would spend more time educating your mind, you would have less time for self-reflection and would not feel your nerves half so much."

Elizabeth stared down at her plate. Mary was perfectly right, though Elizabeth was rather surprised she chose to point it out so plainly.

"Mary, my dear," Mr. Bennet said, "your mother has been happily feeling her nerves all of her adult life. Nobody enjoys their own nerves better than she does. If she's not to feel them, then who is to take over the task?"

"Listen to your father, Mary," Mrs. Bennet said. "They're my nerves and I can feel them whenever I like. I suppose I can at least be grateful that I am not to be alone on the morrow. A daughter can bring such comfort to a nervous person like myself."

"We look forward to providing you with companionship all the day long, mama," Jane said. "Perhaps we can take the carriage to Meryton."

"The carriage will be quite unavailable tomorrow," Mrs. Bennet said. She avoided Jane's eye as she said, "I'm to send it to fetch Lydia."

Elizabeth looked at Jane with alarm. Mr. Bennet said, "Mrs. Bennet, I would wish you would not be so free with invitations to my home."

"Calm yourself, Mr. Bennet," Mrs. Bennet said. "Your daughter comes alone. Wickham will not be with her. Though I do not see any reason why he should not come."

"No reason but that I don't wish him to be a frequent visitor," Mr. Bennet said. "I received them after their marriage and that is quite enough."

"What cause can you have to keep an amiable son-in-law from our house?" Mrs. Bennet asked. "They are married and Mr. Wickham is charming. You seem quite willing to accept others who are not half so pleasant."

"If you refer to Mr. Darcy," her husband said, "and I can only assume you do, let me remind you that of the two gentleman in question, only one came to ask my permission for the hand of one of my daughters. *That* one has proven a most sensible and genial man and is welcome in this house at any time. The other may stay away if he looks to please me."

Elizabeth was gratified by her father's vigorous defense of Darcy. They had spent enough time together shooting and fishing that Mr. Bennet had begun to value Darcy's true worth. He no longer wondered why Elizabeth had married him.

"Genial, indeed. Never mind, then," Mrs. Bennet said with a note of irritation. "Poor Mr. Wickham does not come, just as you wish. Kitty, this is a most welcome surprise, is it not? I know you miss Lydia as much as I do. I could hardly keep it from you when I got her letter a few days ago, but I was determined to have it a surprise. I thought it would be such fun to have Lydia appear in front of you in the drawing room! Think how diverting that would have been, you would have been so shocked. Well, I suppose I couldn't keep the secret *that* long, but I did keep it a tolerable amount of time."

After dinner was blessedly over, Mr. Bennet asked to see Elizabeth in the library. He leaned back in his chair and said, "It is most inconvenient that Lydia should come just now. I suppose Darcy will be annoyed."

"I suspect so," Elizabeth said, "as I am annoyed myself. She only comes to attempt to squeeze money from Jane and Bingley. She knows there is no hope in pestering me and does not dare say a word to Darcy, but she does think she might wear poor Jane down and she might be right about that."

"Your sister and Bingley are a pair," Mr. Bennet said. "They are delightfully kind, and yet I sometimes think they ought to have someone in their employ whose sole job is to say no to all comers. It would save them a deal of money."

"But sir," Elizabeth said, "then they would feel very sorry for the poor chap that was to be the naysayer and direct him that he wasn't to make himself too uncomfortable and he should say yes when it seemed easier."

Mr. Bennet laughed. "And what of you, Lizzy? Are you still as happy as when I saw you last?"

"Even happier, I think. I find that my husband and I deepen our understanding of each other day by day." Elizabeth blushed to express her feelings so directly, but what she said was true. She and Darcy had delighted in discovering how much their minds thought alike, as well as where they did not. Darcy was able to point out when a thing might be taken more seriously than Elizabeth took it, and Elizabeth was able to point out when a thing might be taken *less* seriously than Darcy took it and so they tended to reach a rational and moderate decision on most questions. Georgiana was delighted with the new gaiety that now filled Pemberley and had herself grown not quite as serious and reserved as she had been. It was a happy household and Elizabeth was determined to keep it that way.

"I am glad for you, Lizzy. It is just as a marriage should be. I must presume your happiness does not at all depend on your husband bringing back any game," Mr. Bennet said. "He is a remarkably bad shot, though I would never point it out to him."

Elizabeth bit her lip to stop from laughing. "Please do not point it out to him. As for me, it has been thoroughly explained by my husband, and Mr. Bingley, too, that the pheasants who inhabit the environs of Pemberley are a clever lot who will not allow themselves to be found."

"And does he account for the pheasants here, which he also seems to have difficulty with?" Mr. Bennet asked.

"Indeed, he does not. Nor do I inquire after it."

Mr. Bennet smiled contentedly, as if all were right in his world. "We must not let Lydia spoil your visit. I will speak to her when she arrives and impress upon her that she is to be reserved in the presence of you girls, and in particular, your husbands."

"That would be very good of you, papa," Elizabeth said, "though impressing anything upon Lydia may be a hopeless case. I shall just endeavor to make sure she does not leave the house with half of Jane's money."

Chapter Three

The following morning was not altogether comfortable. Mrs. Bennet could not stop herself from speaking about how she should enjoy seeing Lydia. The carriage had set off at ten in the morning, so Elizabeth expected she should see her sister in the early afternoon. Elizabeth was filled with trepidation about what the following day would bring. Lydia in the same house with Darcy. She wished she could prepare him for it. Elizabeth knew that all his mental preparation before he arrived at Longbourn would be in considering how he would smile at Mrs. Bennet regardless of what ghastly thing she said to him. He would be quite thrown to see Lydia and Elizabeth knew that was when he tended to be at his worst. If he had foreknowledge of some unpleasantness he could face it with equanimity. It was only when he was surprised that he tended to fall back into his mask of haughty disapproval.

Mrs. Bennet had left the sitting room to consult with cook on some matter – everything must be just so for Lydia. Kitty was out in the garden and Mary was locked away somewhere with her books.

Jane said quietly, "As you promised, Lizzy, you will not leave me alone with Lydia? I cannot bear to tell Bingley that I have given away so many pounds for lack of resolve. I know he would not fault me for it, he's too kind for that, but he would be unhappy all the same."

"You have my word," Elizabeth said. "I shall be your merciless banker and not let a crown leave with her."

"I wonder if we judge Lydia too harshly," Jane said. "We have been speaking of her as if we know her scheme, but perhaps she comes for another reason."

Elizabeth smiled at Jane. "Very true. And I have often wondered if the sky would stay blue. Might it not turn green on the morrow? One never knows."

"Yes," Jane admitted. "You are right, of course. I have been engaged in hopeful thinking. I would so wish to think well of her, despite…"

"Do not mind too much. We have only to fend Lydia off today. Our husbands will return tomorrow and then we shall experience one exquisitely awful dinner in which mama will say all manner of rude things about and to Darcy and Lydia will be as bold as ever. We shall get through it, blushing all the way, and then be gone to a happy Christmas at Pemberley."

Just then, Elizabeth and Jane heard the clatter of a carriage arriving outside.

"Lydia!" Mrs. Bennet cried, racing out the door.

Elizabeth and Jane went to the window.

Lydia was descending from the carriage, all smiles. Her dress was overly beribboned, as was her bonnet. Elizabeth thought Lydia had never learned the lesson that too much adornment just looked overworked and self-conscious.

"I suppose we had better go out," Jane said, not sounding very enthusiastic.

"We should," Lizzy said, taking her by the arm. "But I shan't let you out of my grasp."

Elizabeth arrived in the courtyard in time to hear Mrs. Bennet say, "I told your father I did not see why Wickham should not come. We shall miss him so entirely."

"Never mind, mama," Lydia said gaily. "Wickham is quite busy at the moment. Or, he will be."

"Will be?" Mrs. Bennet asked. "He has got a position?"

"I cannot tell," Lydia said. "It's quite a secret. I will only say that we shall be quite well off when he's through."

"Oh I knew it!" Mrs. Bennet cried. "I can guess what it is. Something in the government. I'm sure that is it – Wickham was born to be a politician! Why, one of these days we shall read about him in the newspapers as having made a very great speech."

"Never mind speeches, mama," Lydia said. "I cannot say a word about it so do not ask me. You know how horrid I am at keeping a secret, but Wickham will be positively furious if I breathe a word about it."

Elizabeth and Jane looked at each other. This was good news indeed. Perhaps Lydia would have no further cause to entreat Jane for money. Perhaps Darcy would no longer need to maintain the man.

"Well, sisters?" Lydia said. "Will you greet me?"

"Of course, Lydia," Jane said with real feeling. "It is good to see you."

"How do you do?" Elizabeth said with more reserve.

"Oh look at you, Lizzy," Lydia said in a teasing tone, "you've gone and married Mr. Glum and now you are becoming exactly like him. I feel sorry for you, chained to that dreary person, when Wickham and I have such fun together. Well, we do when we have got the means for fun."

"Lydia," Elizabeth said, "I'll thank you not to begin in such a manner. Keep your opinions of my family to yourself."

"Oh, la, you are getting very prickly," Lydia said. She turned from Elizabeth. "Mary," she cried. "There you are, book in hand as always. You shall never find a man if you don't put those silly things down. Papa says I cannot bring Kitty to live with me, but maybe he shall allow you to come. There is no end of single gentleman we are acquainted with. Where is Kitty, by the by?"

"She's in the garden, dear. Do go see her, she will be so pleased," Mrs. Bennet said. "I meant to keep it a secret, but then it came out. Lizzy was provoking me and out it came. Still, though it's not such a surprise, she will be very glad."

Lydia skipped off to the garden. Elizabeth wished Lydia would not have much time to speak with Kitty alone, but did not see how she was to follow without looking excessively odd. She comforted herself that Kitty was in no danger of going to stay with Lydia and so her influence could only go so far.

Elizabeth and Jane returned to the drawing room.

"Well, Jane?" Elizabeth asked. "Lydia has not changed one bit, but what news! Wickham is to have a position."

"I was most gratified to hear it, but I wonder why the secrecy?" Jane asked.

"I wonder who would give Wickham a position to do anything. I cannot imagine what he could do."

"I suppose we shall find out when they mean to tell us," Jane said.

Elizabeth laughed. "I would be very surprised if we do not find it out tonight. Lydia said herself she is horrid at keeping a secret and that was full of truth. She shall blurt it out before the day is through."

A servant brought in the post and handed Elizabeth a letter.

"For me?" she exclaimed. "Whoever is writing me here?" She glanced at the postmark. "Very curious, it was sent from Hertfordshire."

Elizabeth picked up a letter opener and sliced it open. It was on Pemberley stationary.

'My Dearest Darling –

I imagine you think me ridiculous for writing when we are only to be separated for two nights, but you also know that I do not mind *you* thinking me ridiculous though I should mind it in anybody else. I hope, as well, that as thoroughly as you know me I am able to surprise you on occasion. I wrote this letter before we left Pemberley and had it in my coat pocket all the while we traveled. I have mailed it directly after leaving you at your father's house.

Now, for my predictions. You are sitting very comfortably with Jane somewhere – the garden, perhaps? While I will be by now settled at Hartfield house and should be very happy to converse with my old friend and his very amiable wife. However, I know perfectly well that I am not content. I try my best to enjoy the visit, and give everyone their due attention, yet I know my mind is constantly running off in one direction. What is Lizzy thinking of just now, I will wonder. Is she laughing, as she so often is? Who enjoys her company while I do not? So now you know – your husband is even more ridiculous than you would have supposed. By the end of this visit, Hartfield will no doubt be very glad to send me back to my wife and I will be equally glad to be sent.

All my love,

Fitzwilliam

Elizabeth laid the letter on her lap, more proud of her husband than she had ever been. He was a true romantic at heart and had always been, but it was just recently than he had begun to show it and it was not easy for him. She knew he would have blushed at even conceiving of such a letter, and yet he had done it anyway as he knew she would be pleased.

Before she could at all respond to Jane's enquiring look, Mrs. Bennet burst into the drawing room waving a sheet a paper. "You'll never guess, Lizzy. You will not either, Jane. It's from Mr. Collins."

"Mr. Collins?" Elizabeth and Jane said together.

"Mr. Collins," Mrs. Bennet said, as if she had a bad taste in her mouth. "And the man is inconveniently staying with his father-in-law for some days so as to celebrate an early Christmas. He wishes to call on us and pay his respects. So he says, anyway," she said with a sniff. "More likely he's come to take inventory."

Elizabeth took the letter from Mrs. Bennet's hand and read it aloud to Jane.

My dear Mr. and Mrs. Bennet,

I have the pleasure of just now visiting Sir William and Lady Lucas at Lucas Lodge. My wife was very eager to see her parents over the holiday season, but a man of my profession must have a very great many commitments at this time of year. I must be ready to deliver a moving and erudite sermon on Christmas day and then we will be expected to dine at Rosings. As you will recall, my benefactress, Lady Catherine, depends upon my company most decidedly and could not possibly make do without me. That, at least, is my assumption as she very recently said to me, Mr. Collins, you will dine here Christmas day. Knowing how much Lady Catherine desires my presence and knowing how much my wife desires to see her family, I determined that we should come to Lucas Lodge early. By this method, we shall make everyone happy who is so desirous of our company.

I will call on the morrow and I trust I will find the family well. Time heals all wounds, as they say. Of course, some wounds are more easily healed than others so I will not be shocked should I find you still in the throes of despair over your daughter Lydia, though you managed to get her married in the end. I would consider it a duty to provide you with some comfort during this trying time.

Sincerest Regards,

William Collins

Elizabeth dropped the sheet of paper and stared at Jane.

"I've sent a note back and asked him to dine with us tomorrow," Mrs. Bennet said. "Get the whole thing over with faster."

"But why?" Elizabeth cried. "Why would you ask him to dine tomorrow? Darcy and Bingley will be here and you know--"

Mrs. Bennet cut her off. "What I know is that I have no intention of going through the whole ceremony with Mr. Collins. First he calls, then we are obliged to call, then we are asked to dine, then we must ask him to dine – days upon days of Mr. Collins. No, it would be far more convenient to get the invitation out of the way while we are to have a large party in the dining room anyway. Oh, don't stare openmouthed at me, Lizzy, I know what you're thinking. Your poor husband cannot hold up against it. Well, Mr. Collins is his own aunt's protégé after all. If he finds Mr. Collins so trying, then he should talk to the great Lady Catherine about it. I'd put my own word in if I knew the lady."

First Lydia, now Mr. Collins? It would be too much for Darcy, she wouldn't subject him to it. She would meet him at the end of the drive and tell him to keep going, for his own good.

Mrs. Bennet stalked out of the room. Elizabeth stared at the sheet of paper, now lying on the carpet.

"Mr. Collins," Jane said softly.

"Mr. Collins and Lydia," Elizabeth said. "If I should wish to entirely vex my husband I could not have put together a better party."

"Perhaps mama is right, Lizzy," Jane said hopefully. "It will be a large party. I'm sure she has invited Sir William and Lady Lucas too. And then Charlotte will be here. Dear, rational Charlotte."

"Yes," Elizabeth said. "Dear Charlotte. Darcy likes her very much. But can one rational female offset the evils of both Lydia and Mr. Collins? I think it is too much to hope for."

"Do not forget," Jane said, "there is myself and Bingley. Just as you would shield my money from Lydia, so we will form a wall around Darcy."

Elizabeth smiled gratefully. "Who shall we hear of next?" she said, in more of her natural playful tone. "I expect Lady Catherine will sail through the door at any moment, and then our party will be complete."

The following day brought rain and Elizabeth by turns hoped that Darcy and Bingley had decided to put off their journey, or if they did not, that they should come through it safely. Jane fretted at the window.

"Bingley is very susceptible to colds, you know," she said to Elizabeth.

"My Wickham has a stronger constitution than that," Lydia said. "Of course, he was a soldier, so he would have. I don't suppose your Bingley has ever lived in a tent surrounded by thousands of men? That is just how it was at Brighton."

"He shall be alright, Jane," Kitty said. "He's a man of sense and I'm sure he would not do anything dangerous."

"I agree with Kitty," Elizabeth said. "Both of our husbands are men of good sense. It will not surprise me one bit if we should get a letter that they have delayed the journey for a day or two until the roads dry out."

"One's constitution may change over time," Mary said. "I believe a great many factors may affect it."

"Mrs. Forster and I had such fun," Lydia continued, "making our way through a sea of tents to see dear Wickham."

Elizabeth and Jane studiously ignored this reference to their brother-in-law. Elizabeth was pleased to see that Kitty seemed embarrassed by it. Only Mary seemed oblivious. She said, "I wonder how much a healthful diet may affect one's constitution? It seems likely. I will see if I can find something on the subject."

"Yes, Mary," Elizabeth said, wearily. "Do." Privately, Elizabeth determined that when she brought Mary to Pemberley she would positively ban her from the library. It was well that a girl chose to be well-read, but Mary had taken to hiding herself between the pages of one dull volume after the next. It was no surprise that she was not at her ease when conversing with people – one could not practice conversation with a book.

"Lydia," Elizabeth said, hoping to interest Jane enough to leave the window, "tell us of this new scheme of Wickham's. I know you pretend it is a secret, but you know perfectly well you have never kept a secret in your life. You might as well be out with it."

"La, Lizzy," Lydia said, "I should so like to tell you all. Wickham is so very clever, you would not believe it."

Elizabeth thought that unlikely. Wickham could be charming when he liked, but clever? She did not think so.

"I will only say that is a remarkable scheme and it is to make our fortune," Lydia said, "and if some in this family are lucky, it will pay them handsomely too."

"Some in this family?" Elizabeth asked. "Lydia, you do not propose to ask anyone in this family to finance some scheme of Wickham's?"

"I do not propose to ask anyone anything," Lydia said. "Do not bother scolding me, Lizzy. Anyhow, I cannot tell you anymore about it. Wickham impressed on me quite determinedly that he would be very angry if I did, so I shan't."

Darcy kept his head down against the driving rain. They had passed through Meryton and were finally coming close to Longbourn. It could not be too soon for Darcy's wish. He had missed his wife and so had determined to go out into this weather. Hartfield had urged him to delay the trip until the following day, but

Darcy would not be put off. Bingley had been equally impatient to go and they had encouraged each other until they had made themselves believe it was a sensible decision. After hours of rain and mud and the wind whipping his face, Darcy had conceded to himself that it had not been at all sensible. They would both be lucky is they did not come down with cold.

"We're nearly there," Darcy shouted, turning his head to Bingley.

He looked around him, but all he saw was an empty road and the trees that lined it bending in the wind.

"Bingley," he yelled. "Bingley, where are you?"

The hour for dinner arrived. The Lucas' carriage had rolled up to the door with their son-in-law in tow, but there was still no sign of Darcy and Bingley. It was decided amongst them all that the men must have decided to delay their trip. After all, the ride to Hartfield was nothing on a fine day, but with the rain coming down in sheets the roads would be very bad indeed. Sir William remarked that they had set off especially early though they had such a short distance to travel so that they might go carefully through the weather. It was no day to be out on horseback.

Elizabeth prayed the men had indeed delayed their trip. She could be comfortable if she could believe Darcy in front of a fire and only worrying what she should think when he did not arrive. She was less comfortable imagining that he was by the side of the road somewhere with a lame horse.

The party had gathered in the dining room and Elizabeth found herself next to her father, with Mr. Collins at the other end of the table. She was well-pleased with the arrangement, though Mrs. Bennet did not look so pleased to have Mr. Collins so nearby herself.

"Mr. Collins," Mr. Bennet said. "I would hope you still enjoy the devotion of your patroness, Lady Catherine."

Elizabeth stared at her father. She knew exactly what he was doing and it was entirely for his own amusement. As if to catch a fish, he had thrown out a line with a shiny and colorful fly tied to the end of it. Now, all he had to do was sit back and wait for the fish to bite. As diverting as it promised to be, Elizabeth rather wished her father would forgo such amusement for the sake of her friend Charlotte.

"Sir," Mr. Collins said, in his usual ponderous manner, "I have the honor of informing you that my relations with Lady Catherine remain what you have known them to be. She depends upon my counsel and we receive the great complement of being invited to dine at Rosings at least twice a week."

"Indeed they are invited continually," Sir William said, "at least twice a week and sometimes more. I have seen it with my own eyes. My daughter regularly rubs elbows with one who has been to St. James. Excepting myself, of course, who she has known since she was a baby and who has also been to St. James, so that makes two. It is a noble place, St. James."

Elizabeth knew perfectly well that her father would ignore Sir William's allusions to his own visit to St. James. Everyone in the neighborhood was too well acquainted with it.

"And I recall," Mr. Bennet said to Mr. Collins, "that you were a devotee of the carefully crafted complement. The type of complement that might sound as if it had been just thought of in the moment."

"Unstudied," Mr. Collins said. "Unstudied is how I would describe it. It is what I always aim for, as the unstudied complement has an elegance to it that the *studied* complement can never have. Only last week I happened to mention that there are those that have the mark of nobility upon them for all to see. They hardly need speak to let people know it, as it is all in their countenance. I had been working on something along those lines for above two months. Of course, Lady Catherine understood my meaning perfectly and was well-pleased. She is a woman of great understanding--"

Charlotte broke in. "Lady Catherine is always very civil. Elizabeth, I remarked to her on the grace and beauty of Pemberley."

Poor Charlotte, Elizabeth thought. Always racing ahead to avert her husband's words before he said something too ridiculous and never able to be quick enough.

"Indeed," Mr. Collins said, glancing disapprovingly at Lydia, who had just yawned loud enough for all at table to hear. "Lady Catherine was most gratified to hear of Charlotte's impressions of Pemberley. Of course, we all lamented the ill-timing of the visit. The Bishop was to come to Rosings that very week! Had it been any other week I should have been able to go to Pemberley myself." He addressed Elizabeth directly and said, "Naturally, I will apologize to Mr. Darcy if there has been any slight felt in my not appearing."

Charlotte blushed, as she had very cleverly chosen that week, and that week only, as the one in which she would come to Pemberley. Elizabeth had been given the impression that Charlotte had told her husband that Darcy had insisted on that week and no other, though he had done nothing of the sort. Darcy approved of his wife's life-long friendship with Charlotte and had declared he would be willing to put up with Mr. Collins for a week so that Elizabeth might have the pleasure of her company. Though he had declared it, Elizabeth knew he had been much relieved to find that the man would not come.

"I'm sure no such apology is necessary, Mr. Collins," Elizabeth said. "I'll venture to say it was hardly felt."

"Lady Catherine mentioned that she had not visited the place in many years," Mr. Collins continued, "but was certain of an invitation arriving from her nephew at any moment."

Elizabeth inwardly groaned. She knew they would have to ask Lady Catherine eventually, though she had hoped to put the visit off as long as possible. That was no longer a possibility now. She must issue the invitation directly after Christmas. There had been a thaw in their relations once Lady Catherine became thoroughly convinced that Elizabeth was indeed Mrs. Darcy and planned to stay that way forevermore. Elizabeth supposed she dare not overly try the lady's patience.

"She is quite reconciled to the marriage, you know," Mr. Collins said to the air. "Naturally it was a blow, for so many reasons. Miss de Bourgh being foremost of course, and then there was the general question of the suitability of the connection. Still, Lady Catherine has borne up quite admirably."

Mr. Bennet stared at Elizabeth, seeming delighted with Mr. Collins' speech.

"Yes," Elizabeth said, "She has been a regular soldier about it."

Charlotte sat looking at her hands. Elizabeth suspected that Mr. Collins was far easier to manage in Hunsford, as he was not so daring in his speech in the presence of Lady Catherine. Now that he was set loose upon Hertfordshire, catching him was rather like trying to take down a greased pig. A person might corner him in one direction just in time to see him set off in another.

"And you, sir?" Mr. Collins said to Mr. Bennet. "How does your family fare after the unfortunate scandal?"

Lydia dropped her fork.

Elizabeth thought Mr. Collins had hit her father hard on that point. Mr. Bennet was ashamed of what Lydia had done, and for his own part in it. The circumstances around Lydia's marriage had been talked of, and Elizabeth was certain that many of the facts of the case were known. No doors had been shut to Darcy and Bingley and, in consequence, to herself or Jane, but the circumstances had been talked of. Elizabeth thought that if she had married less brilliantly, she would have felt the effects far more than she did. The real test would come when Kitty was out in society. Kitty had no fortune to wrap around herself as a protective haze of pounds and percents. She must just stand on her own. Would doors shut against Kitty to pay for Lydia's crime?

"I see that Mr. Wickham is not welcome at this table," Mr. Collins said. "I am pleased to know that, at least. It is exactly what Lady Catherine has wished to hear."

"Mr. Wickham is certainly welcome at this table," Lydia cried. "He is only not here because he is too busy with other things."

Mr. Collins stared at Lydia. "If that is true, then I think we may congratulate ourselves on our fortunate timing. I could not, as Lady Catherine de Bourgh's most trusted advisor, sit down to dine with such a man."

Charlotte had laid her hand on her husband's arm, a look of alarm spreading across her features.

Lydia stood up. "*You* could not sit down to dine with *him*? Listen here, you pompous windbag, Mr. Wickham would not be interested in dining with you, because you are a complete bore. Charlotte, I do not know how you don't murder the man while he sleeps. Nobody would fault you for it."

"Lydia!" Elizabeth said. "That is quite enough. Leave the room this instant."

"Gladly," she said, and flounced out.

An uncomfortable silence descended on the table.

"Well, Mr. Collins?" Mrs. Bennet said, looking pleased at her daughter's outburst. "You see my daughter bites back. Best not to tease her."

Before Mr. Collins could respond, Fitzwilliam Darcy strode into the dining room. He was dripping wet from the rain and had a serious look on his face.

"Bingley has disappeared," he said.

Chapter Four

Elizabeth leapt from her place at the table and raced to her husband. "You are soaked through," she cried.

"That is of no consequence," Darcy said.

Jane sat stone still. "What can you mean, my husband has disappeared?" she asked.

"I lost him on the road," Darcy said. "I do not know how. One moment he was directly behind me, the next he was gone. I backtracked to the last place where I had turned to speak with him, but could not find any trace of him."

Jane's face had gone a sickly white. "Lizzy," she said, and then fell into a faint. Mr. Bennet caught her before she fell to the floor.

Poor Jane! To hear such news! Her nerves were delicate to begin, but she was with child. They must be more so now.

"Take Jane upstairs," Elizabeth said. "You," she said, pointing at Mr. Collins, "help my father. Charlotte? Will you follow and see that my sister is made comfortable? Mama, send a servant to fetch the doctor. Sir William, perhaps you will retire to the library – my father will join you there shortly."

Mr. Collins rose and bowed to Mr. Darcy. "I am at your service sir, and I will venture to convey Lady Catherine's complements to her nephew and your complements back to her. You may consider me, sir, your willing messenger."

Darcy stared at Mr. Collins as if he were some strange creature just emerged from the forest.

Charlotte pulled her husband's arm and sent him to Mr. Bennet to help carry Jane upstairs. "I will see that she's alright, Lizzy, depend upon it," Charlotte said.

Elizabeth gave Charlotte a grateful look. All but Mrs. Bennet and Kitty had dispersed.

"Bingley missing?" Mrs. Bennet said, still seated at table. "I never heard of such a thing. How does a person go missing? Most extraordinary."

"Mama," Kitty said softly, "let us leave Lizzy and Mr. Darcy alone. Remember, we must send for the doctor for Jane." Kitty skillfully steered her mother out of the dining room.

"You must get changed," Elizabeth said. She grasped Darcy's hands together in her own. "You are freezing."

"There will be little point in getting changed now," Darcy said. "I must go back out. I only stopped here to change my horse and see if I might not rouse a search party."

"And so you have," Elizabeth said. "I shall go out with you."

"You!" Darcy cried. "No, my darling. I would not have you risk it. The conditions of the road are very bad. You might take a fall, or catch cold."

"But you must allow me, you see?" Elizabeth said. "Who else should go? I am a far better horsewoman than anyone else here."

"But certainly there is…well I could ask…"

"Ah, you see? No names come to mind. Mr. Collins and Sir William would be useless. One can barely sit a horse and would send you his complements as he slid to the ground, the other would fill your mind with imaginary tales of St. James. My father is only in the habit of riding as far as his nearest covey. Further, you require someone who knows this neighborhood well. That leaves only myself."

"I had rather go out alone than risk your health," Darcy said.

"I am sure you had rather," Elizabeth said. "But then I suspect that you would go missing too and then I should be forced out alone, searching for two men instead of one. Further, you know I am more likely than you to know where a rider might go astray. Was the rain coming down particularly hard when you lost sight of Bingley?"

"It was, though it is less so now," Darcy answered.

"And where were you when you last recall seeing him?"

"We had just passed through Meryton," Darcy said.

"It is as I thought," Elizabeth said. "There are all sorts of paths a horse might choose in the middle of a heavy rain. Bingley, not being able to see very far ahead of him, likely left the horse to pick its own way through."

"I pray you are right and we should have him safe in front of the fire before the night is through," Darcy said. "Very well, Elizabeth, your points are well taken and, as I have no confidence in my ability to stop you, you shall come with me."

"Well said, husband, a very gracious defeat. I shall just run up and check on Jane and we will be on our way in a moment."

Elizabeth ran up the stairs and entered Jane's room. Jane was awake, but pale against the white linen pillowcase. Her sister was surrounded by nurses. Charlotte sat next to the bed, while Lady Lucas and Lydia debated the best treatments for fainting.

"Mama has sent for the doctor," Lizzy said. "At least, she should have done by now."

"Do not concern yourself with me, Lizzy," Jane said. "It is Bingley that is in real danger."

"You are not to worry, Jane," Elizabeth said. "I've had it from Darcy that they had just passed through Meryton. You know as well as I how many paths a horse might take in that neighborhood. Darcy tells me the rain was coming down hard and so my own prediction is that Bingley allowed his horse to choose for itself and it chose wrong. The rain has tapered and Darcy and I are to go out in a moment. We shall have your husband back as quick as you like."

"You are going out with Darcy? Do be careful, Lizzy!" Jane said.

"Indeed, do," Charlotte said.

"Bah," Elizabeth said. "Who else should go but me? Rest easy, Jane. Darcy and I will sort this out directly."

Elizabeth left the sickroom wishing she could feel as confident as she sounded. The roads, she knew, would be treacherous. While it was only raining, the air was cold and there might very well be ice in spots. As for Bingley, she dearly hoped he was only lost and not thrown from his horse and lying in a ditch. It was no weather be out in, especially if a person were injured.

She flew down the stairs and grabbed Mr. Bennet's greatcoat from a peg. It was far too big, but it would keep her warm and dry. She could hear her father with Mr. Collins and Sir William in the library. She thought to tell them she was going, but then thought better of it. Let them discover she and Darcy had already gone and they would not be able to put forward any complaints on the dangers.

Darcy waited for her where she had left him. He eyed her coat, which hung down to the ground and covered her hands.

"I have looked better, I know," Lizzy said with a smile.

Darcy pushed up her sleeve and grabbed her hand. "I think not. You look a brave woman willing to face the elements for your friend Bingley and your sister."

"Let us go," Lizzy said. "If Bingley is hurt it will do him no good at all to be out of doors a moment longer than is necessary."

Darcy nodded and they set off to the stables. They passed the kitchen, where Mrs. Bennet was giving directions to a servant about bringing the doctor. He was to take the carriage as the doctor would never come out in such weather if he were expected to come on horseback. They slipped by unnoticed, careful not to make a sound as they went by the doorway.

They hurried down the long hall that led to the back of the house. As soon as Darcy opened the door leading outside, Elizabeth felt the chill of the wind. The rain had let up but still came down in a cold mist. The moon was full at least, and most of the clouds were driven off.

The stables were quiet, but upon entering the building the horses began to grow restless. Elizabeth knew they would be made anxious by this surprise visit. Horses liked nothing so much as predictability and they would be nervous to see anyone at such a late hour.

Darcy saddled a horse from the team that had pulled one of the Pemberley carriages. Elizabeth saddled King Lear, her father's horse. King Lear was a steady and even-tempered horse and Elizabeth knew him well. He would be well-suited for the strange ride they were about to take.

Darcy gave her a leg up and mounted his own. "Shall we backtrack along the road to Meryton in case Bingley has found his way back to it? If we do not see him, we can begin down the paths you spoke of."

Elizabeth nodded and they set off.

The road was by turns dark and light as clouds raced across the moon. The wind blew sporadically and in different directions, as if unsettled as to what it meant to do. Darcy's horse whinnied and sidestepped at the moving shadows around them. King Lear was imperturbable and plodded along as if his only concern was when they should return to the stable and have done with this nonsensical trip.

The road toward Meryton was narrow and lined with hedges, with an occasional break through them. Elizabeth was sure Bingley must have turned down a path. Had he stayed on the road they must certainly have come upon him even if he had been thrown. The lights of Meryton came into view, looking as so many winking and blinking lights through the trees.

"It was here that I last saw him," Darcy said, reining in his horse. "I had turned to him and said we should be at Longbourn within the quarter hour. It was raining so hard that I cannot say with any certainty that he heard me. But, he was behind me, that I know. Only a few minutes later I turned to say something else and he was gone."

Elizabeth considered the location. There were indeed a variety of paths to take, as she had taken most of them from Longbourn to Meryton many times. Most eventually encountered a farmer's stile, which must halt the horse. If Bingley had been thrown, they must find the horse to have any sense of where he might be.

She chose the most well-worn path as one likely to confuse a horse. "There," she said, pointing to the right side of the road. "You see how the road itself curves. If one were to continue straight on, one would end up on that path. It's nearly as wide as the road so if one did not know the area, it would be difficult to see that one had gone astray."

They turned their horses and set off down it, taking turns calling out for Bingley. Elizabeth thought their shouts into the darkness had any empty sound. She listened closely for any reply but heard nothing over the wind blowing through the trees.

After winding down the path for a quarter mile they came to a field. Elizabeth knew there was a stile on the far side of it and a horse could not have gone further.

"He is not here," she said. "Bingley has not come this way."

They made their way back to the road and chose another path. And then another and another. The sky lightened to gray and it became not so difficult to see around them. They searched and called, but saw no sign of Bingley. It was as if their friend had vanished. As the sun came up they found themselves back on the road once more.

"There are no more likely paths, are there?" Darcy asked.

"None that I know of," Elizabeth admitted. "And I believe I know them all."

"Perhaps he has made his way to Longbourn," Darcy said. "He could easily have missed us on his way as we have spent most of the night off of the road."

"Perhaps," Elizabeth said.

"Come, you are tired, my love," Darcy said. "It is time for me to take you home. If Bingley has not arrived ahead of us, I will rouse a search party in Meryton and comb the entire county."

The sun had risen and reflected on the wet grass. The air was cold but the fog began to burn off. It would be a fine day.

Elizabeth and Darcy rode in silence, each deep in their own thoughts. King Lear quickened his pace when he realized they were heading toward the stable and not down another path. Elizabeth was certain the horse was both tired and disgusted. She felt rather the same.

Elizabeth thought of what she must tell Jane. They had not found Bingley. She prayed Darcy was right and they should find him at Longbourn with an amusing tale of mishap and adventure.

Mr. Bennet stood in the courtyard, evidently anxious for their return. Elizabeth knew immediately that Bingley had not arrived. It was written over her father's features.

"You did not find him," Mr. Bennet said.

"No," Darcy said, "and I conclude he has not been here either."

Mr. Bennet shook his head. "I have kept servants on the lookout all night. We have seen no one."

"I will go to Meryton," Darcy said, "and see if I can raise a search party."

"You shall do no such thing," Mr. Bennet said. "I will go myself. The two of you have been out all night and must go to bed, at least for some hours. I know who may be called on to give assistance and you do not."

Elizabeth was grateful for her father's decisiveness. She did not know how Darcy would have been able to continue after the journey from Hartfield and then an all-night search for Bingley. As well, and what her father helpfully didn't mention, was that half of Meryton no doubt still held a low opinion of Mr. Darcy. Though Wickham had been exposed, that did not entirely undo the general perception of Darcy's haughtiness. Elizabeth could hardly imagine the reaction if her husband were to go through town asking for assistance.

"If you are determined," Darcy said to Mr. Bennet.

"Very determined," Mr. Bennet said. "Dismount, I'll take the horses to the stable and be off myself. I'll raise a party and we'll begin the search immediately. I'll send word on how we go on. You'll not have to face anyone in doors, everyone is still abed."

Darcy leapt down from his horse and helped Elizabeth down.

Mr. Bennet led the horses away. Darcy held Elizabeth's hand and took her inside.

Elizabeth wondered if she should see Jane, but decided that her sister was better left sleeping. She and Darcy crept quietly up the stairs so as not to rouse anybody. When they got to their bedchamber, she got out of her damp clothes and wrapped herself in a robe. She lay down and rested her head on Darcy's shoulder.

"Jane is pregnant," she said quietly.

"He knows," Darcy said.

They both fell into a restless and troubled sleep.

The sun was high when Elizabeth woke. Darcy was already awake and half-dressed. They said nothing. They often communicated in silence. Neither Elizabeth nor her husband were in the habit of filling the air with useless conversation and there seemed nothing to say at this moment. They both were certain that Bingley had not yet been found. The house was too quiet, as if it were in mourning already.

Elizabeth hurriedly dressed and they went downstairs. Elizabeth found Jane and her mother in the drawing room. "Has papa sent any news?" she asked, sitting next to Jane and holding her hand.

Darcy bowed to Mrs. Bennet and sat down.

"Only that he has raised over twenty men and they have set off in all directions," Jane said. "They are using my aunt's house as a sort of headquarters and Mr. Philips is keeping a map of which areas have been searched and which have not."

Lydia skipped into the room. "Well? Where is Mr. Bingley? I supposed he's told you all about his adventure."

"He has not yet been found," Elizabeth said.

"Oh," Lydia said quietly.

Darcy stood up. "I will go to your aunt's and see where I may search that they have not already done."

Elizabeth nodded. She briefly thought of joining her husband, but there were already so many searching and she knew that Jane had need of her.

Darcy left and Jane said, "Oh, Lizzy! What could have happened to him?"

"I do not know," Elizabeth said. "But I feel sure that with so many men, and daylight to help, he will be found soon enough. For all we know, he discovered he was lost and spent the night in a haystack somewhere and is now turned around as to where he is. He never did spend very much time in the county, after all."

"I wonder if he hasn't gone to Netherfield," Mrs. Bennet said.

"Mama," Elizabeth said, watching Darcy canter down the drive, "You know Bingley no longer has the lease of the place."

"I'm sure I do not understand *that* at all," Mrs. Bennet said. "It was a fine house and so convenient to Longbourn. But even so, he must have fond memories of it."

"Wherever Bingley is," Elizabeth said, "we can be certain that he is somewhere. We will find him, Jane. Now, I will ring for tea."

Silence fell over the drawing room. Jane twisted her hands but otherwise presented a composed appearance. Elizabeth could not imagine what she would be doing at this moment if it were Darcy, and not Bingley, who were missing. It seemed such a miracle that they had come together in the end. Everything and everybody, including herself and her husband, had worked against it. After all that, to wonder if happiness were being snatched away through an accident of fate?

A clatter of hooves sounded on the drive. Elizabeth and Jane both leapt up from their seats. "It must be news," Elizabeth said, looking out the window.

A rider on a tall bay horse cantered toward the house. Elizabeth did not recognize him, though it was hard to see his features as he wore a hat pulled down low. He rode up to the front door, but instead of dismounting, he threw a rolled-up paper at it, turned and rode away.

"What on earth," Mrs. Bennet said, peering out the window.

Elizabeth ran to the door and flung it open. The man had disappeared, but the paper he had thrown lay on the ground. She picked it up and quickly opened it, praying it was the news that Bingley had been found. Lydia had followed her and peered over Elizabeth's shoulder.

To whom it may concern:

Charles Bingley is held for ransom in the amount of ten thousand pounds in coin. You will have two days to gather it. It shall be left inside the barn at Holbrook Farm before sunset. If anyone makes an attempt to stake out the location, you will not see your friend again. Do as we ask, exactly as we ask it, and your friend will be returned unharmed.

Chapter Five

Elizabeth's mind raced as she reread the letter. Ten thousand pounds! Whoever these men were, they must have known that Darcy accompanied Mr. Bingley, as he was the only man of Bingley's acquaintance who could afford such a sum. Had they somehow known Darcy and Bingley would pass a certain spot on the road and then attacked Bingley? Elizabeth supposed it could be possible that Darcy had not heard it. It had been raining and the wind blowing hard. But what a daring scheme! They could not have predicted the weather would work in their favor. What would they have done if it had been a fine evening and Darcy had been able to put up a fight? And how had the kidnappers even known where the two men would be?

Lydia had taken in a sharp breath upon reading the note and fled up the stairs.

"What is it, Lizzy?" Jane asked, coming up behind her.

Elizabeth handed her the note. As much as she might want to shield her sister from it, she knew she could not.

Jane read the note, growing paler by the second. Her hand dropped and she said, "I knew it. I was certain something terrible had happened to him, and it has."

"Well," Mrs. Bennet said, coming into the hall. "Is he found?"

"He is not," Elizabeth said. "Take Jane back to the drawing room. I must ride after Darcy with no delay. He did not leave long ago and I'm certain I can catch him on the road to Meryton." She took the note from Jane. "He will need to see this."

Elizabeth directed one of Darcy's horses to be saddled. King Lear was steady, but she would need a faster horse. As she waited impatiently for it, she reread the note again. Who were these men? Was this some sort of criminal business – kidnapping gentlemen and then demanding money for their return?

Elizabeth paused. She had heard of something similar when they had been in London. An acquaintance had told her of a gentleman in Suffolk who had disappeared the year before. The family had received just such a demand, but not for nearly so much money. It had been paid and the gentleman had been returned. He could not describe his kidnappers as they had all worn masks. It had been rumored that the whole thing had to do with a gambling debt, though the gentleman swore it was not so.

The groom led a chestnut horse out into the yard and helped her mount. Whatever this was, she needed Darcy. He would know what to do.

Elizabeth tucked the note in her dress, galloped down the drive and headed toward Meryton.

It was a fine day and the sun was high. Elizabeth rode her horse hard, determined to catch Darcy before he went off searching somewhere.

Where had the men taken Bingley? They would not have taken him to Holbrook Farm. It was currently unoccupied as the old tenant had died the year before, but they would not have given it as the location to drop off the money if Bingley were there at this moment. They must have another place somewhere. Something out of the way, where nobody would notice anything unusual happening. As well as Elizabeth knew the neighborhood, she could not think of such a place.

She came around a bend in the road and spotted Darcy's tall figure ahead. She called out to him and he wheeled his horse around.

Elizabeth reined in her horse.

"Why have you not stayed with Jane?" he asked.

Elizabeth handed him the note. "This is why."

She gave him a moment to read it, then said, "What are we to do? Where can they be holding him? I've searched my mind for some likely place but can think of nowhere."

"They may be far from here," Darcy said. "In fact, I think it likely. It would be too dangerous to keep their captive nearby."

"But Darcy, have you heard of this before? When we were at the Cranby's, Mr. Bradincote told me of a gentleman in Suffolk who suffered the same. Have you heard of others?"

"None, but one instance some years ago in Derbyshire. The man was returned after a ransom was paid, but it was never discovered who had done it."

"They ask for ten thousand pounds," Elizabeth said quietly. "I must think, from that outrageous amount, that they knew you would be here. Bingley could not afford such a sum in ready money."

"No," Darcy said thoughtfully, "he could not. But as you said, I can."

He moved his horse closer to Elizabeth and touched her cheek. "I will ride to London this instant and see my banker. Though it grows late in the day, it is but twenty-four miles off and I will easily arrive before sunset. I believe the kidnappers have seen all of this ahead of time and that is why they give us exactly two days."

Elizabeth was at once relieved and frightened. To carry such a sum of money on the road? It would be dangerous.

"I can guess at what you are thinking," Darcy said. "I will return in a carriage and bring footmen from the London house to act as guards. There is a pistol in the house and I shall bring that too. I could not, in any case, carry that much coin on horseback. I assume they ask for coin and not bank notes so that they cannot be traced."

Elizabeth was a little mollified by the plan, though still fearful of her husband carrying so much money.

"Nothing," Darcy said in a determined voice, "absolutely nothing, will keep me from coming back to you in time. Then, we will do exactly as the note directs. I see no point in risking Bingley's life over a sum of money. Let them have what they want and we will get what we want – our friend back safe among us."

Elizabeth nodded.

"Now," Darcy said, "return to Jane. Assure her that Bingley is well. Whoever these men are, they will be sure to keep their captive well. They intend on absconding with the money and that is all they want. They will have no wish to be pursued for a murder."

"I had not thought of that," Elizabeth said, "but I think you must be right. Go, and I will take care of my sister."

"I think it would be well to keep this note private," Darcy said. "I know we should tell the search party to halt their effort, but I fear that if all of Meryton knows of the kidnapping, some among them may decide to be heroic and do something that puts Bingley in more danger than he is already. Perhaps we should put it about that we have had word of him and a search is no longer necessary. We might say he had reason to go to London unexpectedly and we have just discovered a note he left at Longbourn. It would be odd, to be sure, but I do not know what else we could say."

Elizabeth bit her lip. "All of Meryton already knows of the kidnapping."

"How can that be?" Darcy asked, looking surprised.

"Because my mother knows," Elizabeth said. "She will have said something in front of the servants, who now make their way to

Meryton via various paths. Our housekeeper, Mrs. Hill, is no doubt ahead of all of them."

Darcy sighed. "Very well. Perhaps you had better go on to your aunt Philips house and let them know what has happened before they hear it from a merchant."

"I will," Elizabeth said.

Darcy leaned over and kissed her. "Until tomorrow." He wheeled his horse around and rode toward London.

Elizabeth turned her horse toward Meryton and her aunt.

Her aunt Philip's house had been transformed into a bustling headquarters. Mr. Philip's had pinned a map to the wall and had written various notes upon it. Elizabeth could see that much of the area had been searched already.

Men were coming and going and nobody had yet noticed Elizabeth. She hoped to find her aunt and speak with her privately.

A man brushed by her and strode to her uncle. "You'll never believe it," the man said. "I just had it from Mrs. Hill that Mr. Bingley has been kidnapped!"

"Idle gossip, I'm sure," Mr. Philips said, his back to the man as he wrote more notes on the map. "Mrs. Hill is fond of a good tale."

"I am afraid not, uncle," Elizabeth said.

Her uncle turned around. "Elizabeth! Can you mean it?"

"I do," she answered. "I would ask that you call off the search party and thank the men very kindly. But please, uncle, ask that they do nothing further. Mr. Darcy has things well in hand and any interference would be, well it could be dangerous."

"Upon my word," Mr. Philips said, "I am very sorry to hear this. Very sorry indeed. Mr. Bingley is such a nice fellow, never met anyone friendlier. I will of course tell the men that nobody is to go off trying to solve the crime on their own."

"Thank you," Elizabeth said. "Now, I must return to Jane."

Elizabeth found her parents, Jane, Kitty and Mary waiting for her in the drawing room. She went to Jane and said, "Darcy is on his way to London even now. He will return on the morrow with the ransom. He says he shall do just as the note directs and is sure that Bingley is being well-cared for. I think he's right, Jane. These men only want money and to get away. They will not harm Bingley."

"I will hold on to that hope, Lizzy," Jane said. "I have no other hope so I must cling to that."

"Darcy is a generous man," Mr. Bennet said. He looked at Elizabeth and said, "As we have known for some time."

"He certainly is the only man we know who could afford it," Mrs. Bennet said. "What is ten thousand pounds to him anyway?"

"It is a great deal of money to anyone," Jane said. "I am just grateful that my husband has such a loyal friend."

"Friendship is peculiar to the human condition," Mary said. She did not continue with that particular line of speculation when she noticed Elizabeth glaring at her.

"Darcy assured me that nothing will prevent him from returning in time," Elizabeth said.

"I wish I had known his plan," Mr. Bennet said. "I would have offered to accompany him."

"He would not have allowed it, papa," Elizabeth said. "He was determined to set off immediately."

Mr. Bennet nodded. "No doubt King Lear and I would have slowed his progress in any case."

"Mr. Bennet," Mrs. Bennet said, "I will not have you involved in any kidnapping scheme. Remember, one false step and then you die and then Mr. Collins moves in and what would become of me and Kitty and Mary? I suppose we could move in with my sister, since it seems we would not all be welcome at Pemberley. Some would be welcomed at Pemberley," she said, looking at Kitty, "but some would not. Perhaps I could pitch a tent somewhere."

Mr. Bennet, seeming to wish to avoid another long and pointless conversation about the entail, rose and left the room. Elizabeth suspected that her mother had broached the subject on purpose and that this was her new method for driving her husband from the drawing room.

Elizabeth sat with Jane and held her hand. "Do you feel quite all right?" she asked softly. "Physically all right. Because, you know…" As far as Elizabeth knew, Jane had not told anyone else of her pregnancy. Elizabeth supposed she should not have told Darcy, but then he had already known of it from Bingley himself. She briefly thought to tell Jane of the exchange but then decided not.

"Yes," Jane said. "I am all right." In a whisper she said, "I told the doctor of my condition, he says I have nothing to worry about but I should try to keep my nerves calm."

Elizabeth nodded, though that sounded like very silly advice. How did one keep their nerves calm when their husband was missing? As Elizabeth searched her mind for something encouraging to say to Jane, her sister said, "Where is Lydia?"

"I do not know," Elizabeth said. "I saw her last when we received the note."

"She said she had a headache," Kitty said, "and has gone to lie down."

Elizabeth supposed that was just as well. Lydia would not be much help in a situation such as this anyway.

"Jane," Elizabeth said. "I understand that this type of kidnapping is not all that uncommon. While we were in London, Mr. Bradincote told me of one such case. Darcy told me of one other he knew about. Both were resolved peacefully and the gentleman returned unharmed. I think we must look to that for encouragement."

"Indeed," Jane said. "But what keeps troubling my mind, Lizzy, is who would know where and when to find Bingley and Darcy on the road. Someone knew of their plans. I hope it is nobody connected to us, such as a servant. I do not know all of Bingley's servants overly well, and you of course, must not know half that work at Pemberley. I just hope there is not a traitor living in one of our own houses."

"Perhaps you have hit upon something, Jane. If, indeed, it was a servant who set up the plot, it would not likely be one of ours. They are too far away and could not know Darcy and Bingley's schedule so exactly. Hartfield's servants, on the other hand, *would* know as they would have seen Darcy and Bingley depart. We do not know that house, it could be they have recently hired someone who they do not know well, and that person saw an opportunity and took it."

"It could very well be," Jane said. "That would account for them being able to waylay Bingley on the road with such precise timing."

"Only," Elizabeth said, "it does not account for how they knew that Holbrook Farm was unoccupied. Though I suppose they could have come the day before and discovered it. I will relay our suspicions about Hartfield's servants to Darcy when he returns."

Elizabeth thought her husband must be getting close to the city by now. He would have ridden his horse hard for ten miles or so and then changed to a fresh horse to continue on. At the speed he was likely travelling, the trip would not take long.

She imagined him arriving at the house in town and firing off orders. One to fetch his banker, one to alert Jemmings and prepare for the return trip to Longbourn. Another house might be sent into chaos by the unexpected arrival, but Jemmings and his staff of footmen would take the whole thing in stride. Darcy had told Elizabeth that in his bachelor days he changed plans often and

Jemmings could never be certain when he might turn up. He was always ready for the unexpected.

If Elizabeth guessed right, the cook would want to make Darcy an elaborate meal but he would forgo it and just order a plate of cold meat and cheeses. He would take a glass of port into the library after dinner and stare into the fire as he had so often done at Pemberely. She had always joined him there and occupied herself with reading and they would stop their various activities from time to time to talk. Once, she had put her book aside and asked him what he thought about while he watched the flames. He had said, "I think about how lucky I am to be so content and wish the same for everybody." She knew that was not what he would be thinking on this night. He would be planning out each step that needed to be taken, beginning with his banker. Just how large was ten thousand pounds in coin anyway? Elizabeth would not be surprised if it did not take up half the carriage.

Elizabeth hoped they could all be content again. She wished they could be just as they were. Jane had not long had happiness with her husband, and now there was a baby to come. Darcy must get Bingley back.

Chapter Six

Darcy lay on his bed staring into the dark. As he had noticed at Hartfield, it felt strange and uncomfortable that Elizabeth was not by his side. The two kept separate bedchambers at Pemberley, as that was expected, but they did not sleep apart. For Darcy, there was nothing sweeter than waking in the morning to his wife's sleepy smile and her hair in a tumble. Elizabeth said she was sure the servants were shocked that they carried on like a couple of farmers who had only one bedchamber between them, but Darcy couldn't see his way clear to caring what the servants thought. He might have cared a year ago, but he had not been happy then.

A year ago, he had been drifting from one ball or house party to the next, uncomfortably aware whenever he was in the presence of a lady who had set her cap on him. He knew he should marry, and there had been many who would have been suitable, but he had not been able to bring himself to do it. His aunt had been determined to marry him to Miss de Bourgh, though Darcy had told her repeatedly that it would not be so. Caroline Bingley had attached herself to his side most decidedly, but all he could ever envision with her, with them all, was a future of cold civility. It had depressed him more than he had even realized. It had seemed that all he had to hold on to was protocol and tradition and rank. It had never made him happy, but it had always made him feel secure.

Then he had arrived at Netherfield. It was to be just another trip into yet another county, this time to indulge Bingley in his wish for an estate. He had looked around the country ball that first night and thought of all the crude advances he would have to dodge, of all the eager mothers he would have to escape. Until he realized that there was one there who did not find him so fascinating as Caroline Bingley and her ilk had always pretended to find him. One for whom fifty thousand pounds held not much interest. One who seemed to think he was rather a bore than anything else. Who was this creature with the lively eyes?

His own interest had grown until he found himself in the most awkward position – wanting to marry a woman that all of his faculties told him was unsuitable. He had no illusions about it, Caroline had seen to that. She took every opportunity to abuse Elizabeth and her family. Darcy could not discount all of what Caroline said – Mrs. Bennet was indeed dreadful. The younger sisters were not much better and Mr. Bennet seemed to tolerate it all without the slightest idea of curbing their more outrageous behavior. Everything was against the match.

Everything was against the match, but he could not help brooding on it. Elizabeth Bennet was not to be forgotten, though he dearly wished it could be so. Finally, he had indulged himself and made the offer anyway, and what an offer he had made. He still cringed to think of it, of Elizabeth staring him straight in the eye as she said: And you call yourself a gentleman? He had been so blinded by ideas of rank that he had failed to be what he had always thought himself, a gentleman.

He had no need to cling to rigid ideas of rank and tradition anymore. Let the servants think what they like about he and Elizabeth's failure to sleep in separate bedrooms. If they were compared to a couple of farmers, then Darcy found he was happy to be a farmer.

Darcy knew Bingley to be equally blessed. Jane was so different from Elizabeth, but then Bingley was so different from Darcy. His old nanny used to say 'there's a lid for every pot' and he supposed that was true. He and Bingley had both been lucky enough to find their right match.

What must Jane be going through at this moment? Darcy could hardly imagine what he should be like if it were Elizabeth missing. All Jane's happiness rested with Bingley. If anything were to happen to him she would be utterly crushed. And with child, too. How could she bear it? How could Elizabeth bear it to see her sister thus. How could Darcy bear it to lose his closest friend?

"I must get Bingley back," he said softly.

The evening passed quietly, but for Mrs. Bennet's fretting.

"I do not see why a kidnapper should single out Mr. Bingley," she complained. "He's the most amiable man alive.

Perhaps they do not know that about him. But why should they come to Hertfordshire anyway?"

Elizabeth could not determine if her mother was most upset that Bingley should have fallen prey to criminals or that he had not been there for dinner.

Elizabeth had insisted that Jane retire early. It could do her no good at all, especially in her current state, to stay up late with worry. Her sister had said she had rather not sleep alone. It would help her be less fidgety if Elizabeth were nearby. Elizabeth climbed into bed with Jane. She blew out the candle and said, "Darcy will return on the morrow and we will have your husband back among us and this will all seem like a bad dream."

"I'm frightened, Lizzy," Jane said into the darkness.

Elizabeth did not say so, but she was frightened too.

Elizabeth was up with the dawn. She slipped out of the bed, careful not to wake Jane. She knew it would be an endless and tense day ahead. Elizabeth did not know how long it would take Darcy to make the arrangements in London. How did one go about amassing ten thousand pounds in coin anyway? She supposed she shouldn't fret about it. Darcy said he would return with the money and so he would. Once her husband made a promise, it was a certainty.

The house was quiet. Mrs. Bennet and her sisters were not likely to be awake for some hours. Except for Jane. Elizabeth did not think her sister would stay abed long. Her sleep had been restless throughout the night and Elizabeth sensed that Jane had not been sleeping soundly when she left the room.

Elizabeth slipped down the stairs and went to the library. She knew she would find her father there, as he was an early riser and enjoyed his quiet mornings. Elizabeth had spent many a morning of her youth sitting silently by him as they both read or watched the day coming alive outside of the window. It had been their own private time of companionship. Mary had once asked Elizabeth why their father was so disposed toward her. Elizabeth had explained that it was because she rose early and did no talking.

Mr. Bennet was in the library, but not in his chair where Elizabeth would have expected to find him. Rather, he paced the length of the room.

He saw his daughter and said, "I feel as if, once again, I do nothing. My own daughter is in distress, my own son-in-law has been kidnapped, and it is Mr. Darcy taking charge of everything. What can I do, Lizzy? I have a great urge to do something."

"There is nothing to be done at present," Elizabeth said, taking her father's arm. "We must just wait for my husband to return."

"Ah," Mr. Bennet said, "now, you see, that sort of direction, do nothing, is exactly the sort of thing I used to like. Why do something when it would be easier not to? Why rein in a daughter when Colonel Forster and Brighton might do it just as well? I find I am no longer comfortable with that mode of going on."

"Do not blame yourself further for Lydia, papa."

"But I must," Mr. Bennet said. "I have done Lydia a great disservice. Did I tell you I apologized to her?"

"You did not," Elizabeth said, surprised. She would not have thought anyone owed Lydia an apology. Quite the opposite, in fact. She was still waiting for Lydia to apologize to *her*.

"I can see you are surprised and do not fault you for it. She nearly ruined you all and that must be deeply felt. But, Lizzy, consider this: if one were to raise a child on the streets of London and provide no education or trade, would one be so very surprised that the child becomes a pickpocket? I have done the same with Lydia. I provided no education, no direction and then I am to be surprised that she has so little understanding? It is not just this running away with Wickham, you know. We have all been too quick to pretend that now that they are married, all is right with the world. It is not. I must take responsibility for the idea that I have ruined one of my daughters forevermore. Lydia will never be as she ought, and it is entirely my own fault."

Elizabeth had never heard such a speech from her father. There were no jokes or self-deprecation. Only a cold and hard assessment of his actions. She could not say he was entirely wrong. Elizabeth supposed she ought to herself consider more generously why Lydia was who she was. Lydia really hadn't had any guidance. Was that to be laid only at her father's door? She and Jane had been older and had a superior education and had seen quite clearly where Lydia had been heading. Perhaps they had not envisioned that she would go so far as to run off with a man, but for years they had deplored their sister's behavior. What had they done about it? Very little, Elizabeth was forced to admit.

"It was not only you, papa," Elizabeth said. "Jane and I saw what was happening, how her character was developing, and did little about it."

"But you did come to me, Lizzy, and beg me not to let her go off to Brighton," Mr. Bennet said. "Would that I had heeded your advice."

Elizabeth colored. A sudden realization had come over her. For so long, she had been satisfied with herself in regards to Lydia. As her father said, Elizabeth had sounded the alarm. She had known the trip to Brighton could only lead to trouble. She had convinced herself that her understanding and her actions had been superior to the rest of her family. She saw now that had not been the case.

"Papa," Elizabeth said, "since Lydia ran off with Wickham, I have congratulated myself on that very point. I knew the trip could not be wise. But I find, after listening to what you have had to say, that I should not have congratulated myself so much. What did I ever do to help mold Lydia's character up to that very moment? Very little, I am ashamed to say. If we go to your analogy of the pickpocket, then all I did the day I came to you to urge you not to let her go to Brighton was stand in the doorway and shout, "Look, that child is going out to pickpocket." I did little beforehand to ensure that it would not be a foregone conclusion. I have thought I was satisfied with my actions, when in truth I have only been satisfied with my ability to guess the future."

Mr. Bennet smiled. "I do not think it was ever your responsibility to raise Lydia. But, I suppose I am not such a changed man that I won't be happy to share the fault around to whomever wishes to share in it. I am most comforted, though, by the idea that we shall save Kitty. And Mary too, should she ever need saving. One wonders if our Mary will ever put down a book long enough to need saving, but we shall see."

"I am determined to do my best for both of them," Elizabeth said. "and I think I shall try to be more understanding of Lydia from now on. I cannot approve of her, at least not yet. She is too unrepentant for that. But I will try to be more generous in spirit, if not in pocket."

"I have apologized to Lydia," Mr. Bennet said. "and I am certain she did not understand a word of it. But I owe no such apology to Wickham. I know it pains Lydia that I do not welcome the man to this house, but that is where I must draw the line. He was let in once after the marriage, for propriety's sake, and that will be enough."

"A very sensible line it is, papa," Elizabeth said. "Should you let him in, you might find you had a hard time getting him to go out again. I expect they would both very much enjoy a free house and their meals taken care of."

"Dinner with Mr. Wickham every night?" Mr. Bennet said. "No, not even I deserve that punishment."

Mr. Bennet and Elizabeth both felt that all that should be said had been said. They sat in front of the window and watched the day come alive.

Darcy signed papers at a furious pace while his banker stood in front of the desk. They had been in conference earlier that morning and Darcy had learned that no single bank could deliver so much coin on such short notice. Mr. Gambole had leveraged his every relationship in the city to piece together the ten thousand pounds.

The front door knocker sounded. Mr. Gambole said, "That will be the first of the deliveries. By the end of it, there won't be a coin left in London. You are certain this is the right mode of recovering your friend?"

"It is the only mode," Darcy said. "I won't risk my friend's life trying out some scheme to outsmart the criminals. It's only money, you know."

Mr. Gambole looked deeply shocked at the statement. Darcy smiled, of course his banker would be shocked to hear somebody say it was only money. The man lived and breathed pounds and pence.

The door knocker sounded again. Another delivery had arrived.

"It almost feels," Mr. Gambole said, "as if I am making to throw ten thousand pounds into the Thames."

"I can absorb the blow," Darcy said. "You know I can."

"You most certainly can," Mr. Gambole answered. "Though you would find yourself in difficulty if you were to pay a ransom every year."

"I will presume it will not come to that," Darcy said. "I think we can be assured this is a one-time event."

"I think you will not mind if I advise my other clients of this strange circumstance, assuming I do not mention names. I would wish to put them on their guard, especially when traveling. One cannot know where these scoundrels may strike next."

Darcy nodded. The door knocker sounded again. For all Mr. Gambole's fretting about giving away ten thousand pounds, the man was a model of efficiency. All Darcy had to do was wait for it all to come in, load the carriage and be off. He had met with Jemmings and the footmen earlier. They knew the situation and what they were to do. Jemmings had helpfully offered to round up more pistols. Darcy had not asked from where. Jemmings had helpfully mentioned that he was a crack shot. Darcy had not asked how he came by the skill. Jemmings could solve any problem put to him and his master had always thought it best not to enquire to closely as to how any particular thing was accomplished. Jemmings had come into his father's employ as a boy and Darcy remembered his father saying that he had come from a rough upbringing. Jemmings had watched and learned and picked up the mode of speech and way of doing things of the butler he served so many years ago and, over time, he had risen in the ranks. Darcy suspected that, for all his polish now, he could still go underground in London and deal with any scoundrel to purchase anything a person might require.

When the carriage set off for Longbourn, it would be guarded by four armed footmen and a sharpshooting butler.

Elizabeth peered out the window, as she had done half the morning. She knew that Darcy could not arrive so soon, but felt compelled to watch for him anyway. Instead of seeing the blessed sight of her husband's carriage, she saw Mr. Collins striding toward the house. The only compensation for a visit from Mr. Collins is that he brought along his wife.

He was let into the drawing room and began his speech immediately. Elizabeth assumed he had been practicing it for some hours.

After bowing to the ladies, he said, "I am most grieved that you have not yet been able to recover your friend, Mr. Bingley. In times of such trouble, you have only to turn to your clergy for comfort. Lady Catherine always says that a clergyman cannot take on too much of another's troubles. Though she does feel, and rightly so I believe, that the troubles should not interfere with one's dinner. There are rarely such troubles as that. I suppose I should wonder what she would make of the current case, but as I wrote her all about it yesterday, I feel I will not be on tenterhooks long to know her views. She will write me her opinion most expeditiously."

Mrs. Bennet rolled her eyes and muttered, "Why do we care about Lady Catherine's opinions, I wonder. Though the lady seems to have no shortage of them."

Charlotte left her husband's side and took her place next to Elizabeth and Jane. "I would say anything to comfort you, Jane, if I only knew what."

"It comforts me to have you here," Jane said. "I feel a very great need for friends at this moment. I can hardly contain myself while waiting for Mr. Darcy's return and all that must be got through today. To think, just days ago I did not have a care in the world."

"But Bingley will be got back," Elizabeth said. "He will."

The three sank into silence. Mr. Collins had cornered Kitty and was espousing his views on a variety of subjects. Mrs. Bennet had avoided his company by pretending she was suddenly called from the room to address a housekeeping matter, though no such summons had arrived. Lydia was casually backing away, but poor Kitty was absolutely cornered.

Lydia joined them on the sofa and whispered, "La, Charlotte, he does like to lecture."

Elizabeth could see that Charlotte was deeply annoyed. Her friend said nothing, however.

"Now Jane," Lydia said, "you must stop being so sad. I'm sure when Bingley gets back he will tell you it was all a big lark. You shall laugh like anything."

"Laugh?" Elizabeth said. "Lydia, how could you say so?"

"I just say that it shall come out right and all this fretting will have been for nothing."

"I appreciate your attempt at…comfort, Lydia," Jane said. "But it is entirely useless. I can only presume you would yourself be in a state if it were Wickham that had been taken."

Lydia colored and said, "Nobody would make off with Wickham, he has nothing to take. Some, who might have helped more, have been on the stingy side."

Elizabeth used all her self-control to hold her tongue, and then only for Jane's sake. She had told her father that she would be more understanding of Lydia, but the truth was her sister was infuriating.

"Do not look at me so, Lizzy," Lydia said. "The truth is, Mr. Darcy is up in London this very minute collecting ten thousand pounds that he won't miss for a moment."

"Thank the heavens my husband is doing just that," Elizabeth said.

"My dear," Mr. Collins said, having allowed Kitty to escape from him, "I am certain you wish to remain with your friends. For myself, I must begin composing my Christmas sermon. It is the most important sermon of the year and I must make it stern, yet inspiring. Interesting, yet not entertainment. Joyful, yet not fun. It will need just the right tone. I will go for a walk and it will all come to me."

As Mr. Collins took his leave, Charlotte said, "Mr. Collins finds his work easier when he is surrounded in nature. He spends a great deal of time in the garden in Hunsford and I do encourage it."

"I suppose that old dragon at Rosings approves, then," Lydia said. "Wickham tells me she is absolutely awful. Nobody is to move a finger without Lady Catherine's consent."

"Lydia," Elizabeth said sternly, "not every thought you have needs to be spoken. Some, in fact many, of your thoughts should stay where they are and be known only to you. Leave us alone, you do no good here."

Chapter Seven

Darcy stepped into the carriage. Jemmings climbed in after him, armed with two pistols. Four footmen rode outside, equally armed. Jemmings had been gone from the house for under two hours and had returned with enough weaponry to arm a militia. Darcy thought if highwaymen were to attack the carriage it would be the unluckiest day of their lives.

As the carriage barreled out of London, Darcy thought through what must come. The carriage was filled with canvas bags of coin. He was to take them to Holbrook Farm before sunset. This, he could not do alone on horseback. The kidnappers must know that. He could not in any way carry all of it on a single horse. He must take the carriage all the way there. He had determined to hide Jemmings inside of it in case there was any trouble.

He would arrive at least two hours before sunset and so would make the deadline well in time. But what then? Would Bingley be at the farm, or returned in some other fashion? If he would be in the barn, tied up in some manner, was he there even now? Darcy hoped he could count on Mr. Philips to keep the men of

Meryton well away from the area. He could not afford the risk of the criminals becoming nervous.

Jemmings had told Darcy quite a lot of what could be expected when dealing with the criminal element. Darcy had kindly not inquired into where Jemmings had come by the information. One thing his butler had said weighed on Darcy's mind. A cornered criminal was a dangerous criminal.

"It shall all come out right, sir," Jemmings said. "We'll see to that. These sorts of people are not too smart. Nobody that's got a working brain risks their neck on a regular basis."

"I hope you are right, Jemmings," Darcy said. "I don't know much about those sorts of people."

Jemmings winked and said, "I got their number, sir. Now, seein' as how we'll get there with time to spare, my advice is we stop at Longbourn first and then continue on our way to that farm where we're to make the drop . We'll want to know if another set of directions arrived. These kind of criminals are always second-guessing themselves. We got to make sure we're going to the right place. As well, we can leave the footmen behind. You drive the carriage and I'll hide inside. I'll only come out if I hear trouble. That's the way to get on with the thing all smooth-like."

Darcy nodded. Jemmings really was a marvel. Darcy had not considered that a further communication might have arrived or what he should do with the extra footmen.

"Here they are!" Elizabeth cried, watching Darcy's carriage clatter up the drive. She ran from the window and met it outside. Darcy jumped down and grasped her hands. "You are well?" he asked.

"Yes, of course. It is Jane who suffers. Have you got the ransom?"

"I have," Darcy said. "I won't come in, I only stopped to find out if any further communication had been received. Jemmings thought there was a risk that they might change the location."

"No, indeed, we have received nothing," Elizabeth said.

Jane had come out of the house. She looked at Darcy, but seemed incapable of saying anything.

Darcy went to her. "All is well. You are not to worry. I am going this minute to get Bingley."

Jane nodded.

"I must leave my footmen here," Darcy said. "If you could see that they are taken care of. Except for Jemmings. He'll come with me."

"I know you will be very against the idea," Elizabeth said, "but I think I should come as well. Do you even know the location of Holbrook Farm?"

"I do know it," Darcy said. "It is the only farm between here and Lucas Lodge. A lane leads from the road up an incline and then down again to the house and the barn. I have been thinking that is why they chose the spot – not only is it vacant, but it cannot be seen from the road."

Elizabeth sighed. Darcy knew *exactly* where it was. She had hoped his unfamiliarity with its location would be a reason for her to go. She found she could not stand waiting and doing nothing. She knew it was what she should be doing, what any sensible female would be doing, but it was not what she *wanted* to be doing. She had rather face down a hundred kidnappers than spend one more moment in the drawing room.

"I cannot allow it," Darcy said. "I really cannot. I would wish to give way to every of your inclinations, and mostly I do. But not in this."

Elizabeth was silent. She knew Darcy was right, she just did not like it.

"My darling, if anything were to happen to you…" Darcy's voice had become low and husky, a tone Elizabeth recognized well. He only sounded such when he was deeply moved. She felt a sudden wave of guilt wash over her. She must not consider her own inclinations at such a moment. She could not upset him, he had too much to accomplish on this day.

"You are right," she said in a lighthearted tone. "As a rule, I prefer not admitting myself in the wrong and so you are not to become hopeful that this will become a habit. However, I will admit myself wrong in this case." She squeezed his hands and said, "Go on, be very, very careful and do not give another thought to me until you are back safe."

Darcy climbed onto the carriage while Jemmings hid inside. He turned the horses and headed down the drive. He was both relieved that his wife had not pressed him to come, and proud that she had even had the idea. There was not a braver or more stalwart woman in England.

The lane that led to Holbrook Farm was not a quarter mile from Longbourn. Darcy glanced at the lump that lay next to him on the seat. A pistol hid under an old horse blanket, ready to fire if he should need it. He dearly hoped he would not need it, as if he did it meant that things had not gone as planned. As well, he had little faith in his ability to shoot, though he comforted himself that a man would be a bigger target than a pheasant and so might be more easily hit.

He turned the horses into the lane that led to the farm. As he trotted up the incline he braced himself for what he might find when he crested the top. Would there be an ambush of some sort? He did not think so. He was well convinced that these men were after money only and would not want to involve themselves in further crimes.

Darcy expected he would see nothing, but he was sure there would be eyes watching. If his memory served, he would find the house to the right and the barn to the left. There was a wood not too far behind both and Darcy thought that was where the kidnappers would likely hide. They would want to see him deposit the coin in the barn and leave. He still could not be certain if he would find Bingley there or, if he did not, how they would return him.

Elizabeth paced the drawing room. She had felt herself all nerves over the past two days, but that had been nothing. All this while she had fretted over how Darcy got on, but except for the fear that he carried so much money in the carriage he had not been in any real danger. Until now. At this very moment he was heading into a dangerous situation. So this was how Jane had felt all along. Poor Jane! How had she stood it? Elizabeth felt ready to faint with fear.

Dear Darcy. What should she do without him if something were to happen? They were just beginning their life together. They were getting ready for their first Christmas together. Sometime soon, they would have their first child together. She could not bear to lose all the promise of what was to come.

Elizabeth had told Darcy, more than once, that he was the most perfect person in England. He had always laughed heartily at such an idea and, in truth, he was not perfect. He could still be too brooding unless she laughed him out of it. But he was perfect for her.

Darcy crested the ridge and surveyed the farm. He saw nothing in the quiet afternoon but the two buildings side by side. He urged the horses on and was in front of the barn in less than a minute.

He leapt down and raced inside, eager to see if Bingley were there.

The barn was empty but for the smell of hay and horses that had long ago gone. Darcy checked each stall to be certain and even climbed up to the hay loft. Bingley was not there.

There was nothing to do but leave the money, return to Longbourn and await Bingley's return.

Darcy hauled out the bags of coin and deposited them inside the barn, careful to only open the carriage door as wide as necessary so as not to expose that Jemmings was inside. Quite suddenly, he heard –

"My flock will know, because they know *me*, how seriously I take my duties on this holiest of days. Piety and charity are the words to live by on this day. I would wish to welcome all who are in need to come to the vicarage for plum pudding, though not at dinner time as I will be at Rosings."

Mr. Collins. What was that buffoon doing here?

Darcy looked out of the barn in either direction. He did not see Mr. Collins, but could still hear him shouting out his sermon. He was behind the barn.

He ran around to the other side and found the man pacing and talking to himself.

"Mr. Collins!" Darcy shouted.

Mr. Collins jumped, very much startled to be interrupted in his sermon-composing. "Ah," he said, bowing low, "Mr. Darcy. Your servant, sir. I will take this opportunity to remind you that I remain your willing messenger to my benefactress Lady Catherine."

"What are you doing here, man?"

Mr. Collins began to answer but Darcy realized he would be standing there another ten minutes if he let him go on with it.

"You should not be here," Darcy said. "No one but myself should be here. Have you seen anyone?"

"No indeed, Mr. Darcy. I have been quite alone. I find composing sermons necessitates being alone when one is thinking them up. It is a solitary activity. I tried it in the house once, but my wife said, no Mr. Collins, you'll do better out of doors."

Darcy stared at him. The man was obtuse. In a low voice, he said, "Bingley's captors would have been watching me drop off the money. They sent strict instructions about it and I fear you have put my friend in danger."

"Here?" Mr. Collins cried. "Nobody told me it was to be here!"

"Get in the carriage," Darcy said. "Now."

Mr. Collins ran past Darcy and around the corner of the barn. Darcy squinted, searching the woods for any movement, but saw nothing. He could only pray that Mr. Collins had not frightened off the criminals. In a loud voice he said, "I have complied with your wishes. Ten thousand pounds in coin is in the barn. Return my friend and do not pay any mind to that ridiculous idiot who has been preaching to the trees."

He heard no answer, and could not know if he had been heard. He could only pray that he had.

Darcy returned to the carriage to find Mr. Collins inside of it with a pistol held to his head.

"This fella claims he knows you," Jemmings said, "but I thought I would wait to check on that."

Darcy glared through the window at Mr. Collins. "I have the misfortune of knowing him," Darcy said drily. "If he has been the cause of this scheme failing, I will not mind if your trigger finger slips."

"Mr. Darcy," Mr. Collins cried.

Darcy ignored him and leapt up to the driving seat. He headed the carriage back to Longbourn.

As he approached the road, his thoughts were taken up with what to say to Elizabeth and Jane, what to do next, and how to find Bingley. He would propose to go to Meryton and raise an army and block every road that led out of the area until Bingley was returned. It would be a dangerous move, but now that Mr. Collins had interfered he could not know what the kidnappers might do next. He had been sure that the correct course of action had been to comply with their demands, but he could not be so certain now.

Darcy could hear Mr. Collins complaints behind him. "Sir, there can be no cause for waving that thing around. I can assure you that if it goes off, Lady Catherine de Bourgh will have something to say about it."

"Shut your trap," Jemmings said.

Darcy smiled. Mr. Collins might be used to dining at Rosings and Jemmings might be used to the rougher side of London, but between the two of them, Darcy would take Jemmings any day of the week.

Darcy reached the road and turned the carriage toward Longbourn.

Two men staggered onto the road ahead of him. Darcy reined in the horses and jumped down. "Bingley!" he shouted.

Bingley waved to him and walked forward, helping another man who appeared to be injured. As Darcy ran toward them he suddenly recognized the second man. "Wickham?"

Darcy took Wickham's other arm and helped him toward the carriage, though he was almost reluctant to. There could only be one reason Wickham had appeared so suddenly – he was in on the plot to kidnap Bingley.

"How do you do, Bingley," Darcy said. "Are you yourself injured?"

"Not a bit," Bingley said. "Though I have quite the story to tell."

Wickham seemed to be going in and out of consciousness and his leg was badly bleeding.

"Has he been shot?" Darcy asked.

"Yes," Bingley answered. "And I know what you're thinking, so yes, he was a part of it. But he did not exactly understand what he was a part of until it was too late. I shall tell you all after I see my wife."

"Yes," Darcy said. Jemmings had pushed Mr. Collins out of the carriage and helped to haul Mr. Wickham inside. He ripped his neck-cloth off and used it to tourniquet Wickham's leg.

"He'll do for now, sir," Jemmings said, admiring his handiwork.

"Stay with him," Darcy said to Jemmings. "You are a better surgeon than I."

Darcy shut the carriage door and leapt up to the driving seat. Mr. Collins still stood in the road. "Get out of the way before I run you down," Darcy said.

Mr. Collins leapt out of the way and rolled into a hedge. Darcy slapped the horses with the reins and they galloped to Longbourn.

Elizabeth, Jane and Charlotte stood at the window, lined in a row. They had stood in the very same spot for over a half hour.

All three exclaimed to see Darcy driving the horses at breakneck speed toward the house. He reined them in and Jane let out a cry.

"Bingley!"

Bingley had jumped down from the carriage. Jane was already on her way out the door. Elizabeth breathed a sigh of relief. He had done it. Her husband had saved her sister's happiness.

She paused. Jemmings was dragging someone out of the carriage. Elizabeth leaned closer to the window.

"Elizabeth," Charlotte said, "I believe that is Mr. Wickham, is it not?"

"It is," Elizabeth said. "How stupid I did not see it before."

"See what?" Charlotte asked.

"See that Wickham was behind all this. That's why Lydia thought the whole thing was a joke. She knew all about it."

"Your own sister?" Charlotte said. "I cannot believe it of her. No, Lizzy, there must be more to this tale than we know."

Darcy and Jemmings carried Wickham into the house.

Elizabeth heard Lydia scream from the front hall.

Chapter Eight

The doctor had been fetched and had treated Wickham's wound. The shot had gone clean through his calf and he was in no danger of dying. He might walk with a limp forevermore, but he should easily survive the hit.

Darcy and Jemmings and the footmen had returned to the barn at Holbrook Farm, pistols raised, but the money was gone. They presumed the kidnappers were out of the county by this time and would never be seen again.

Lydia had been dragged from Wickham's side and brought to the library by Elizabeth. There she faced her father and Darcy. Bingley had already told his tale and now sat with Jane in the drawing room. Jane had said that she would no longer allow her husband out of her sight. Elizabeth had been surprised by the force of her tone. It had seemed that Jane had gained a new resolve after this adventure. Bingley had seemed quite content to sit by his watchful guardian.

Elizabeth had been shocked to hear of all Bingley had endured. He had been on the road behind Darcy on that rainy night and very suddenly had been knocked on the head. When he awoke, he found himself locked in a small room. He discovered later that it was a room in the servant's quarters at Netherfield. The house had not yet been taken and so had sat conveniently empty for the kidnapper's use.

A man Bingley did not recognize brought him food and water and he was told that when Mr. Darcy paid up, he would be set free. The conditions were deplorable, but he did not initially fear for his safety. Not until late into the first night, when he had heard an argument erupting in the hall outside of his door. It was between three men and he had been certain that one of the voices had been Wickham's.

Wickham argued that it was never the plan to kidnap Bingley. They only wanted to waylay him for an hour to acquaint him with the business venture. Another man had laughed and said it was exactly the plan to kidnap Bingley. Did Wickham really think they were going to buy a ship and engage in trade when easy money could be so readily had?

Wickham had argued vehemently and swore he would not be party to a kidnapping. When Elizabeth heard that part of the tale she had not been sure if she believed that Wickham had not intended to kidnap. After all, Wickham had nearly kidnapped Georgiana. She would have gone with him willingly, just as Lydia had, but Elizabeth considered their cases different altogether. Lydia was a jaded young lady who had not even particularly cared when she was to get married, Georgiana would have thought she married for love, only to find out later it was for money. Considering Wickham's history, was kidnapping Bingley so far out of character?

What Bingley said next, though, did convince her that Wickham had not known of the plot beforehand. The two other men, Mr. James and Mr. Roker, had attacked Wickham and bound his wrists and thrown him in the room with Bingley. Now they were both captives.

As they sat in the cramped room, hour after hour, Wickham acquainted Bingley with what he had thought the plan was. Always needing money and having no way to get it, Wickham had joined some like-minded men who thought to purchase a ship and go into trade. According to Wickham, it was to be the easiest thing in the world, simply hire an experienced captain and let the profits roll in. They only needed capital to get the venture started and none of the men had it. Lydia had suggested they approach Bingley, but they knew Bingley was with Darcy and could not see a way of speaking with him alone. When Wickham had told the men of the idea, and then told them much more about Bingley and Darcy than he should have, Mr. James came up with the plan to waylay him. At least, Wickham thought that had been the plan. Wickham had not expected the heavy rain and he had not expected that Bingley would be hit over the head. It was supposed to be a diversion. They would stage a carriage accident and tell Bingley and Darcy that one passenger had fallen off somewhere before the carriage actually overturned. This, Wickham thought, would separate the two men while one went back and searched. Wickham was to keep well out of the way until

Bingley was secured alone. Wickham was to claim he had been in the carriage and only going to visit his wife at Longbourn and so make the encounter seem a coincidence. He would then be able to hand Bingley a sheaf of papers outlining the whole business venture. Wickham had been confident in all his facts and figures. He had been confident that Bingley would see that it was a viable plan, and he thought Bingley would want to help his sister-in-law. Bingley, Wickham had been convinced, was a soft touch. A man with too much money and too little backbone. He might finance the thing rather than be continually bothered by Lydia about money. That was what Wickham had thought, at any rate.

During his long hours trapped in the room with Bingley, Wickham began to see that his plan never had a hope of succeeding. Bingley had once allowed himself to be guided by others and it had nearly been his ruin. After nearly losing Jane, he had modified his behavior. He had told his own sister that she was not welcome in his home unless she were to undergo a serious transformation of attitude toward the Bennet family and Caroline was never to advise her brother on any matter again. The only person who was welcome to advise him from here forward was Jane. He had not said as much to Darcy, but only because it had not been necessary. Darcy fully recognized his crime and had been heartily sorry for it. Their friendship had deepened, as Darcy no longer made any attempts to direct Bingley or form his opinions for him. They became equals and liked each other better for it.

Now that Wickham had seen what his two business partners were capable of, he convinced Bingley that they must find a way to escape. He dared not guess what the men might do once they had the money. They might have been willing to let Bingley go, but now that Wickham was on the outs he believed they were both in serious danger. They could not let Wickham go free – he knew far too much about them. If they were to murder Wickham, they would probably murder Bingley too, as they would be afraid of allowing Bingley to go free with the knowledge of it.

The only chance Bingley and Wickham could see was to strike when and if the door would be opened. If the men were intent on murder, they would have to open the door to do it and they would do it before they went for the money. Wickham would charge the man and Bingley was to run.

They heard the key in the lock and Bingley stood behind Wickham at the ready. When the door opened, Mr. James came in with a pistol. Wickham tackled him and Bingley ran. He heard a shot fired. He did not leave the house, however. He knew Netherfield well, having lived there, and took himself to his old dressing room. He knew there was a small window there where he might observe the men leaving the house. When they were gone, he would go down and see if Wickham still lived.

Bingley did, indeed, watch Mr. James and Mr. Roker ride off, and noted with dismay that they took Wickham's horse with them. He had then run downstairs to find Wickham bleeding heavily but still alive. It had been a long walk and they had been careful to stay off the road in case they should run into the two men.

All of that, Elizabeth already knew. Now she would hear what her sister would say for herself.

"It was not supposed to happen like that," Lydia cried. "I know my Wickham, he only wanted to talk to Bingley."

"Why in the world," Mr. Bennet said, "would you and Wickham think that Bingley would invest his money with you?"

"Because, well, Bingley is a softer touch than him," she said, hooking her thumb at Darcy.

"I saw that letter you wrote to Jane," Elizabeth said, "threatening to move in if you did not get money. I will assume that was in preparation for this terrible scheme."

"It was," Lydia said, beginning to get some of her boldness back. "He wouldn't miss the money, we were only going to ask for two thousand pounds, and if he thought he might have done with us for so little trouble, why would he not want to do it? In any case, neither one of us ever talked about kidnapping. We're poor, not criminals."

Elizabeth glanced at Darcy. Providing Wickham and her sister with any further allowance would be quite out of the question now. What would become of them? She supposed she should not care. Lydia certainly had not cared for her sisters' comfort. Not when she ran off with Wickham and not now. Still, now that Lydia was facing real poverty, Elizabeth could not entirely forget happier times. Times when Lydia was very young and ran high-spirited through the house and was always making off with something sweet from the kitchen to share out to everybody. She had been charming little girl, though she was far from charming now. But even so, Lydia was her sister and she had no wish to see her starve.

Darcy's face was grave and Elizabeth could guess what he was thinking. He would have done with the both of them and their names would never be mentioned again.

"You must know, Mrs. Wickham," Darcy said, "that all remuneration from me will be at an end."

Lydia had gone very pale, as if it had just occurred to her that she and Wickham might lose their only financial support in the world.

"It is time for your husband to make his own way in the world. He has thrown away two commissions, and now this. The only thing I can offer you is passage to America and some seed money to get you started. What you both do after that is entirely your concern. Gamble it away, throw it overboard, I care not."

"America!" Lydia cried. "What an idea! I will not go to America."

Elizabeth was shocked at the suggestion, but as she began to think it over it began to make sense. They could not simply go on as if nothing had happened. They could not always wonder what scheme Wickham would think of next, and he *would* think of something. Without the allowance he would only become more desperate and willing to try anything. In truth, Darcy was being overly generous and Elizabeth was sure that could only be for her own benefit.

"I think you should consider the idea, Lydia," Mr. Bennet said. "You will not be welcome in this house again, though I think that is the least of your problems. What has occurred today will never stay quiet. Our own housekeeper is no doubt jogging to Meryton this instant to spread the news. Whatever Wickham's original intentions really were, I do not think a judge would care a fig about them. Should you attempt to stay in England you would likely find yourself transported to Botany Bay. America is a far better choice."

Chapter Nine

It took Wickham three days to be well enough to leave the house. By that time, all of Meryton had heard some version of the story. As Wickham was loathed in the town, the stories that went round were rather more horrifying than the truth. He was made out to be a murderer though no one could say who the victim had been, or a would-be murderer though no one could say who he had thought to murder, or the kind of man who wouldn't blink at the mention of murder, which everyone firmly agreed upon.

Jemmings took Lydia and Wickham to a port. No one, not even Darcy, knew which one. Were they to be questioned about it, they could honestly say they did not know where the couple had fled. Their departure from Longbourn was quiet, but for Mrs. Bennet bemoaning the fact that she should not see her daughter for so long a time and blaming Mr. Darcy for it. Elizabeth did not mention to her mother that it would be unlikely that she should ever see Lydia again.

Darcy and Jemmings had a long conference together before they departed and Darcy was amazed at what could be accomplished when one wanted to disappear. Jemmings would take Wickham and

Lydia to London first and put them somewhere out of the way. He would then, as he told Darcy, 'see the right people' to get papers drawn up that transformed Mr. and Mrs. Wickham into Mr. and Mrs. Hamwick. Should anyone be looking for them on a passenger list, they would not be spotted.

Jemmings was to see that they got on a ship and stayed on it, though Darcy was not at all worried that they might attempt to stay in England. The threat of Botany Bay had been too much for even that hardened couple.

Jane and Bingley had always been nearly inseparable, now they were entirely so. Jane had told Bingley that she was with child on the very day he was recovered. Bingley had admitted to guessing it and would not let Jane exert herself in any way. He had urged that they return to London, rather than make the trip to Pemberley for Christmas, but Jane had overruled him. She would not allow Wickham to spoil such a long anticipated and happy time. If she could come through her own husband's kidnapping she could come through the trip to Pemberley.

Darcy and Elizabeth had joyfully taken the carriages out on Christmas Eve and delivered all of Mrs. Reynold's packages. On Christmas night, it was exactly as Elizabeth had envisioned. Darcy, Elizabeth, Georgiana, Jane and Bingley snug in front of the fire.

Georgiana played on the pianoforte. Jane and Bingley were deep in conference on the other side of the room. Elizabeth sat next to Darcy and he held her hand while no one was looking.

"How do you do, Mrs. Darcy?" he said.

"I do very well, indeed," Elizabeth said.

"Next year," Darcy said, "we shall not stir from Pemberley for Christmas. We shall find ourselves exactly as we are now, with no adventures to recall."

"Next year?" Elizabeth asked. "Oh no sir, next year will be quite different from this."

Darcy sat up. "How so? We are so pleasant here."

"We shall be very pleasant, I think," Elizabeth said. "We shall be right here and very pleasant. Only not just as we are. Next year, we shall have a very small person to entertain and I can assure you that this small person will demand, and get, all of our attention."

"How small is this person, exactly?" Darcy said smiling.

Elizabeth counted out nine on her fingers and said, "So that will be September. We are talking of next December. Still small enough to hold in our arms,"

Darcy heaved a contented sigh. "I am very much looking forward to meeting this small person. This small person will have a most excellent mother."

Kitty came in the new year. It took some time, but it turned out that Kitty had quite sensible instincts. They had only wanted a little encouragement to make themselves known. She became great friends with Georgiana and did and said whatever Georgiana thought was right. Mary followed the year after, but was not as pliable as Kitty. As much as Elizabeth attempted to pry her from her books, on a fine day she could still generally be found in the library.

Still, Elizabeth could not be unhappy with how they were all settled. Three years from Bingley's kidnapping, Elizabeth and Darcy had two young sons and Georgiana, Kitty and Mary were all married. Elizabeth gave Darcy all the credit, as when she was in confinement, it was he that escorted the girl's to endless balls and routs and every other activity he could hardly bear. He did it all with a smile, his only compensation being crawling into bed with Elizabeth, completely exhausted, to relay every ridiculous conversation he had been subjected to. "Did you know," he would whisper in her ear, "that ostrich feathers are out? I only tell you this as Mrs. Astley spent some twenty minutes telling *me*."

Georgiana married a Baron from Sussex. Kitty surprised everyone by accepting an Earl. She was to be Lady Hardeby from now on. That turned out most fortuitously as Lord Hardeby found Mrs. Bennet endlessly amusing. Mrs. Bennet had been bereft at losing all of her girls, but now she gloried in having a countess for a daughter and spent much time at the Hardeby estate. Elizabeth was initially taken aback when a professor from Oxford asked for Mary, but Mr. Bennet pointed out the likelihood of them being happy together and she had to admit he was right.

Lydia was not heard from for two years, but finally a letter did arrive from Mrs. Hamwick to Mrs. Bennet. Lydia and Wickham had settled in Boston and Wickham had gone into the shipping trade after all. Having found himself in the position of having to work or starve, he decided to work. He had been successful and they now lived comfortably with one child and one on the way. No one in their circle in Boston knew of their past and Wickham never again mentioned the name of Mr. Darcy.

Jane and Bingley found an estate nearby to Pemberley and, just as the two sisters had wished, their children grew up as great friends.

The End

Made in United States
North Haven, CT
23 May 2022

19460741R00067